The Innocents

The Innocents

A Story for Lovers

Sinclair Lewis

MINT EDITIONS

The Innocents: A Story for Lovers was first published in 1917.

This edition published by Mint Editions 2021.

ISBN 9781513279237 | E-ISBN 9781513279336

Published by Mint Editions®

 MINT
EDITIONS

minteditionbooks.com

Publishing Director: Jennifer Newens
Design & Production: Rachel Lopez Metzger
Project Manager: Micaela Clark
Typesetting: Westchester Publishing Services

Contents

I

M r. and Mrs. Seth Appleby were almost old. They called each other "Father" and "Mother." But frequently they were guilty of holding hands, or of cuddling together in corners, and Father was a person of stubborn youthfulness. For something over forty years Mother had been trying to make him stop smoking, yet every time her back was turned he would sneak out his amber cigarette-holder and puff a cheap cigarette, winking at the shocked crochet tidy on the patent rocker. Mother sniffed at him and said that he acted like a young smart Aleck, but he would merely grin in answer and coax her out for a walk.

As they paraded, the sun shone through the fuzzy, silver hair that puffed out round Father's crab-apple face, and an echo of delicate silver was on Mother's rose-leaf cheeks.

They were rustic as a meadow-ringed orchard, yet Father and Mother had been born in New York City, and there lived for more than sixty years. Father was a perfectly able clerk in Pilkings's shoe-store on Sixth Avenue, and Pilkings was so much older than Father that he still called him, "Hey you, Seth!" and still gave him advice about handling lady customers. For three or four years, some ten years back, Father and Mr. Pilkings had displayed ill-feeling over the passing of the amiable elastic-sided Congress shoe. But that was practically forgotten, and Father began to feel fairly certain of his job.

There are three sorts of native New-Yorkers: East Side Jews and Italians, who will own the city; the sons of families that are so rich that they swear off taxes; and the people, descendants of shopkeepers and clerks, who often look like New-Englanders, and always listen with timid admiration when New-Yorkers from Ohio or Minnesota or California give them information about the city. To this meek race, doing the city's work and forgotten by the city they have built, belonged the Applebys. They lived in a brown and dusky flat, with a tortoise-shell tabby, and a canary, and a china hen which held their breakfast boiled eggs. Every Thursday Mother wrote to her daughter, who had married a prosperous and severely respectable druggist of Saserkopee, New York, and during the rest of her daytimes she swept and cooked and dusted, went shyly along the alien streets which had slipped into the cobblestoned village she had known as a girl, and came back to dust again and wait for Father's nimble step on the four flights of stairs up to their flat. She was as used to loneliness as a hotel melancholiac; the people they had known had drifted away to far suburbs. In each other the Applebys found all life.

In July, Father began his annual agitation for a vacation. Mr. Pilkings, of Pilkings & Son's Standard Shoe Parlor, didn't believe in vacations. He believed in staying home and saving money. So every year it was necessary for Father to develop a cough, not much of a cough, merely a small, polite noise, like a mouse begging pardon of an irate bee, yet enough to talk about and win him a two weeks' leave. Every year he schemed for this leave, and almost ruined his throat by sniffing snuff to make him sneeze. Every year Mr. Pilkings said that he didn't believe there was anything whatever the matter with Father and that, even if there was, he shouldn't have a vacation. Every year Mother was frightened almost to death by apprehension that they wouldn't be able to get away.

Father laughed at her this July till his fluffy hair shook like a dog's ears in fly-time. He pounded his fist on the prim center-table by which Mother had been solemnly reading the picture-captions in the *Eternity Filmco's Album of Funny Film Favorites*. The statuettes of General Lafayette and Mozart on the false mantel shook with his lusty thumping. He roared till his voice filled the living-room and hollowly echoed in the porcelain sink in the kitchen.

"Why," he declaimed, "you poor little dried codfish, if it wasn't for me you'd never have a vacation. You trust old dad to handle Pilkings. We'll get away just as sure as God made little apples."

"You mustn't use curse-words," murmured Mother, undiscouraged by forty years of trying to reform Father's vocabulary. "And it would be a just judgment on you for your high mightiness if you didn't get a vacation, and I don't believe Mr. Pilkings will give you one, either, and if it wa'n't for—"

"Why, I've got it right under my hat."

"Yes, you always think you know so much more—"

Father rounded the table, stealthily and treacherously put his lips at her ear, and blew a tremendous "Zzzzzzzz," which buzzed in her ear like a file on a saw-blade.

Mother leaped up, furious, and snapped, "I'm simply ashamed of you, the way you act, like you never would grow up and get a little common sense, what with scaring me into conniption fits, and as I was just going to say, and I only say it for your own good, if you haven't got enough sense to know how little sense you have got, you at your time of life, why, well, all I can say is—you ought to know better."

Then Father and Mother settled peacefully down and forgot all about their disagreement.

Since they had blessedly been relieved of the presence of their talented daughter, who, until her marriage, had been polite to them to such an extent that for years they had lived in terror, they had made rather a point of being naughty and noisy and happy together, but by and by they would get tired and look affectionately across the table and purr. Father tinkered away at a broken lamp-shade till suddenly, without warning, he declared that Mother scolded him merely to conceal her faith in his ability to do anything. She sniffed, but she knew that he was right. For years Mother had continued to believe in the cleverness of Seth Appleby, who, in his youth, had promised to become manager of the shoe-store, and gave the same promise to-day.

Father justified his shameless boast by compelling Mr. Pilkings to grant him the usual leave of absence, and they prepared to start for West Skipsit, Cape Cod, where they always spent their vacations at the farm-house of Uncle Joe Tubbs.

Mother took a week to pack, and unpack, to go panting down-stairs to the corner drug-store for new tubes of tooth-paste and a presentable sponge, to remend all that was remendable, to press Father's flappy, shapeless little trousers with the family flat-iron, to worry over whether she should take the rose-pink or the daffodil-yellow wrapper—which had both faded to approximately the same shade of gray, but which were to her trusting mind still interestingly different. Each year she had to impress Mrs. Tubbs of West Skipsit with new metropolitan finery, and this year Father had no peace nor comfort in the ménage till she had selected a smart new hat, incredibly small and close and sinking coyly down over her ear. He was only a man folk, he was in the way, incapable of understanding this problem of fashion, and Mother almost slapped him one evening for suggesting that it "wouldn't make such a gosh-awful lot of difference if she didn't find some new fad to impress Sister Tubbs."

But Mother wearied of repacking their two cheap wicker suit-cases and the brown pasteboard box, and Father suddenly came to the front in his true capacity as boss and leader. He announced, loudly, on the evening before they were to depart, "We're going to have a party to-night, old lady."

At the masterful tones of this man of the world, who wasn't afraid of train or travel, who had gone successfully through the mysteries of purchasing transportation clear to Cape Cod, Mother looked impressed. But she said, doubtfully, "Oh, do you think we better, Father? We'll be traveling and all—"

"Yes-sir-ee! We're going to a movie, and then we're going to have a banana split, and I'm going to carry my cane and smoke a seegar. You know mighty well you like the movies as well as I do."

"Acting up like a young smarty!" Mother said, but she obediently put on her hat—Lord, no, not the new small hat; that was kept to impress West Skipsit, Massachusetts—and as she trotted to the movies beside him, the two of them like solemn white puppies venturing away from their mother, she occasionally looked admiringly up, a whole inch up, at her hero.

II

They took the steamer for Massachusetts at five o'clock. When the band started to play, when Mother feared that a ferry was going to collide with them, when beautiful youths in boating hats popped out of state-rooms like chorus-men in a musical comedy, when children banged small sand-pails, when the steamer rounded the dream-castles of lower New York, when it seemed inconceivable that the flag-staff could get under Brooklyn Bridge—which didn't clear it by much more than a hundred feet—when a totally new New York of factories and docks, of steamers bound for Ceylon and yachts bound for Newport, was revealed to these old New-Yorkers—then Mother mingled a terrific apprehension regarding ships and water with a palpitating excitement over sailing into the freedom which these two gray-haired children had longed for all their lives, and had found during two weeks of each year.

Father was perfectly tremendous. He apprehensive? Why, he might have been the original man to go down to the sea in ships. Mother wailed that all the deck-chairs had been taken; Father found mountains of chairs and flipped a couple of them open as though he were a steward with service stripes. He was simply immense in his manner of thrusting Mother and himself and his chairs and a mound of shawls and coats into the midst of the crowd gathered at the bow. He noted Mother's nervousness and observed, casually, "Mighty safe, these boats. Like ferries. Safer 'n trains. Yes, they're safer 'n staying home in bed, what with burgulars and fires and everything."

"Oh, do you really think they are safe?" breathed Mother, comforted.

Admirable though Father was, he couldn't sit still. He was wearing a decorative new traveling cap, very smart and extensive and expensive, shaped like a muffin, and patterned with the Douglas tartan and an Etruscan border. He rather wanted to let people see it. He was no Pilkings clerk now, but a world-galloper. With his cap clapped down on one side and his youthful cigarette-holder cocked up on the other, and in his buttonhole a carnation jaunty as a red pompon, with the breeze puffing out the light silver hair about his temples and his pink cheeks glowing in the westering sun, he promenaded round and round the hurricane-deck and stopped to pat a whimpering child. But always he hastened back, lest Mother get frightened or lonely. Once he imagined that two toughs were annoying her, and he glared at them like a sparrow robbed of a crumb.

As he escorted her into the dining-saloon Father's back was straight, his chin very high. He was so prosperous of aspect, so generous and proudly affectionate, that people turned to look. It was obvious that if he had anything to do with the shoe business, he must be a manufacturer in a large way, with profit-sharing and model cottages.

The sun went down; Long Island Sound was shot with red gold as little waves reached up hands at the wonder of light. Father and Mother gazed and ate chocolate ice-cream and large quantities of cake, with the naïve relish of people who usually dine at home.

They sat on deck till Mother yawned and nodded and at last said the "Wel-l—" which always means, "Let's go to bed." Father had so inspired her with faith in the comparative safety of their wild voyaging that she was no longer afraid, but just sleepy. She nestled in her chair and smiled shamefacedly and said, "It's only half-past nine, but somehow—." In her drowsiness the wrinkles smoothed away from round her eyes and left her face like that of a plump, tired, happy little girl.

When they were at home Father's and Mother's garments had a way of getting so familiarly mixed that even Mother could scarcely keep their bureau drawers separate. But when they traveled they were aristocrats, and they had entirely separate suit-cases and berths. From the pompous manner in which Father unpacked his bag you would have been utterly beguiled, and have supposed him to be one of those high persons who have whole suites to themselves and see their consorts only at state banquets, when there are celery and olives, and the squire invited to dinner. There was nothing these partners in life more enjoyed than the one night's pretense that they were aloof. But they suddenly forgot their rôles; they squealed with pleasure and patted each other's shoulders fondly. For simultaneously they had discovered the surprises. In Mother's suit-case, inside her second-best boots, Father had hidden four slender beribboned boxes of the very best chocolate peppermints; while in Father's seemly nightgown was a magnificent new mouth-organ.

Father was an artist on the mouth-organ. He could set your heart prancing with the strains of "Dandy Dick and the Candlestick." But his old mouth-organ had grown wheezy. Now he sat down and played softly till their tiny inside state-room was filled with a tumbling chorus of happy notes.

When Mother was asleep in the lower berth and Father was believed to be asleep in the upper he slipped on his coat and trousers and kitten-footed out of the state-room to a dark corner of the deck. For, very secretly, Father was afraid of the water. He who had insouciantly reassured Mother had himself to choke down the timorous speculations of a shop-bound clerk. While the sun was fair on the water and there were obviously no leviathans nor anything like that bearing down upon them he was able to conceal his fear—even from himself. But now that he didn't have to cheer Mother, now that the boat rolled forward through a black nothingness, he knew that he was afraid. He sat huddled, and remembered all the tales he had heard of fire and collision and reefs. He vainly assured himself that every state-room was provided with an automatic sprinkler. He made encouraging calculations as to the infrequency of collisions on the Sound, and scoffed at himself, "Why, the most shipping there could be at night would be a couple of schooners, maybe a torpedo-boat." But dread of the unknown was on him.

Father went through this spasm of solitary fear each first night of vacation. It wasn't genuine fear. It was the growing-pain of freedom. The cricket who chirped so gaily when he was with Mother was also a weary man, a prisoner of daily routine. He had to become free for freedom.

Laughingly, then bitterly, he rebuked himself for fear. And presently he was bespelled by the wonder of the unknown. Beyond the water through which they slid, black and smooth as polished basalt, he saw a lighthouse winking. From his steamer time-table he learned that it must be Great Gull Island light. Great Gull Island! It suggested to him thunderous cliffs with surf flung up on beetling rock, screaming gulls, and a smuggler on guard with menacing rifle. He lost his fear of fear; he ceased to think about his accustomed life of two aisles and the show-case of new models and the background of boxes and boxes and boxes of shoes—tokens of the drudgery that was ground into him like grit. The Father who worried was changing into the adventurous wanderer that henceforward he would be—for two weeks. He stretched out his short arms and breathed deeply of the night wind.

Half an hour later he was asleep. But not, it must be confessed, in the aristocratic seclusion of his own berth. He was downily curled beside Mother, his cheek nuzzled beside her delicate old hand.

III

They changed from steamer to railroad; about eleven in the morning they stepped out at West Skipsit, Cape Cod. Uncle Joe Tubbs and Mrs. Tubbs were driving up, in a country buggy. Father and Mother filled their nostrils with the smell of the salt marshes, their ears with the long murmur of the mile-distant surf, their eyes with the shine of the great dunes and the demure peace of a New England white cottage standing among firs and apple-trees—scent and sound and sight of their freedom.

"Father, we're here!" Mother whispered, her eyes wet. Then, "Oh, do be careful of that box. There's a hat there that's going to make Matilda Tubbs catch her death from envy!"

To the Tubbses, though they were cynical with a hoary wisdom in regard to New-Yorkers and summerites and boarders in general, the annual coming of the Applebys was welcome as cider and buttered toast—yes, they even gave Father and Mother the best chamber, with the four-poster bed and the mirror bordered with Florida shells, at a much reduced rate. They burrowed into their grim old hearts as Uncle Joe Tubbs grubbed into the mud for clams, and brought out treasures of shy affection.

As soon as they reached the Tubbs farm-house the two women went off together to the kitchen, while the men sneaked toward the inlet. Mother didn't show her new hat as yet; that was in reserve to tantalize Mrs. Tubbs with the waiting. Besides, for a day or two the women couldn't take down the bars and say what they thought. But the men immediately pounded each other on the back and called each other "Seth" and "Joe," and, keeping behind banks lest they be seen by young uns, they shamefacedly paddled barefoot—two old men with bare feet and silvery shanks, chuckling and catching crabs, in a salt inlet among rolling hillocks covered with sedge-grass that lisped in the breeze. The grass hollows were filled with quiet and the sound of hovering flies. Beyond was a hill shiny with laurel.

They dug for Little-Neck clams in the mud by the Pond, they discussed the cranberry bog and the war and the daily catch of the traps; they interrupted their sage discourse to whoop at a mackerel gull that flapped above them; they prowled along the inlet to the Outside, and like officials they viewed a passing pogie-boat. Uncle Joe Tubbs ought to have been washing dishes, and he knew it, but the coming of the Applebys annually gave him the excuse for a complete loaf. Besides, he was sure that by now Mother Appleby would be in apron and gingham, helping the protesting yet willing Mrs. Tubbs.

The greatest philosophical theory in the world is that "people are people." The Applebys, who had mellowed among streets and shops, were very much like the Tubbses of Cape Cod. Father was, in his unquenchable fondness for Mother, like Romeo, like golden Aucassin. But also in his sly fondness for loafing on a sunny grass-bank, smoking a vile pipe and arguing that the war couldn't last more than six months, he was very much like Uncle Joe Tubbs. As for Mother, she gossiped about the ancient feud between the West Skipsit Universalists and Methodists, and she said "wa'n't" exactly like Mrs. Tubbs.

There were other boarders at the Tubbses', and before them at supper both of the old couples maintained the gravity with which, vainly, Age always endeavors to impress Youth. Uncle Joe was crotchety, and Mrs. Tubbs was brisk about the butter, and the Applebys were tremendously dignified and washed and brushed, and not averse to being known as superior star boarders from that superior city, New York, personages to whom the opera and the horse-show were perfectly familiar. Father dismissed a small, amateurish war debate by letting it be known that in his business—nature of business not stated—he was accustomed to meet the diplomatic representatives of the very choicest nations, and to give them advice. Which, indeed, he did—regarding shoes. For Pilkings & Son had a rather élite clientele for Sixth Avenue, and Father had with his own hands made glad the feet of the Swedish consul and the Bolivian trade agent.

A man from South Bromfield started to cap the pose, as low persons always do in these boarding-houses, but Father changed the subject, in a slightly peppery manner. Father could be playful with Mother, but, like all men who are worth anything, he could be as Olympian as a king or a woman author or a box-office manager when he was afflicted by young men who chewed gum and were chatty. He put his gold-bowed eye-glasses on the end of his nose and looked over them so wealthily that the summerites were awed and shyly ate their apple-sauce to the last dreg.

Twelve o'clock dinner at the Tubbses' was a very respectable meal, with roasts and vegetables to which you could devote some skill and energy. But supper was more like an after-thought, a sort of afternoon tea without the wrist-watch conversation. It was soon over, the dishes soon washed, and by seven o'clock the Applebys and Tubbses gathered in the sacred parlor, where ordinary summerites were not welcome, where the family crayon-enlargements hung above the green plush settee from Boston, which was flanked by the teak table which Uncle Joe's Uncle Ira had brought from China, and the whale's vertebræ without which no high-caste Cape Cod household is virtuous. With joy and verbal fireworks, with highly insulting comments on one another's play, began the annual series of cribbage games—a world's series, a Davis cup tournament. Doffing his usual tobacco-chewing, collarless, jocose manner, Uncle Joe reverently took from the what-not the ancestral cribbage-board, carved from a solid walrus-tooth. They stood about exclaiming over it, then fell to. "Fifteen-two, fifteen-four, and a pair is six!" rang out, triumphantly. Finally (as happened every year on the occasion of their first game), when the men had magnificently won, Mrs. Tubbs surprised them with refreshments—they would have been jolly well surprised if she hadn't surprised them—and Father played recent New York musical comedy songs on his new mouth-organ, stopping to explain the point of each, whereupon Mother shook her head and said, warningly, "Now, Father, you be careful what you say. Honestly, I don't know what the world is coming to, Mrs. Tubbs, the way men carry on nowadays." But she wasn't very earnest about it because she was gigglingly aware that Uncle Joe was stealing Mrs. Tubbs's share of the doughnuts.

They were all as hysterical as a girls' school during this annual celebration. But Father peeped out of the parlor window and saw the lush moonlight on marsh and field. To Mother, with an awed quiet, "Sarah, it's moonlight, like it used to be—" The Tubbses seemed to understand that the sweethearts wanted to be alone, and they made excuses to be off to bed. On the porch, wrapped in comforters and coats against the seaside chill, Father and Mother cuddled together. They said little—everything was said for them by the moonlight, silvery on the marshes, wistful silver among the dunes, while the surf was lulled and the whole spacious night seemed reverent with love. His hand cradled hers as the hand of a child would close round a lily leaf.

Halcyon days of sitting in rocking-chairs under the beech-trees on locust-zizzing afternoons, of hunting for shells on the back-side shore of the Cape, of fishing for whiting from the landing on the bay side, of musing among the many-colored grasses of the uplands. They would have gone ambling along such dreamland roads to the end of their vacation had it not been for the motor-car of Uncle Joe's son-in-law.

That car changed their entire life. Among the hills of peace there was waiting for them an adventure.

Uncle Joe's son-in-law lived in a portable bungalow a mile away. He rotated crops. He peddled fish with a motor-car. In five minutes he could detach from the back of his car the box in which he carried the fish, clap on a rather rickety tonneau, and be ready to compete in stylish pleasures with the largest limousine from Newport or Brookline. Father and Mother went wheezing about the country with him. Father had always felt that he had the makings of a motorist, because of the distinct pleasure he had felt in motor-bus rides on New York Sundays, and he tactfully encouraged the son-in-law in the touring mania. So it was really Father's fault that they found the tea-room.

The six of them, the Applebys, the Tubbses, and son-in-law and daughter, somewhat cramped as to space and dusty as to garments, had motored to Cotagansuit. Before them, out across the road, hung the sign: Ye Tea Shoppe.

"Say, by Jiminy! let's go into that Tea Shoppy and have some eats," said Father. "My treat."

"Nope, it's mine," said the Tubbses' son-in-law, hypocritically.

"Not a word out of you!" sang out Father, gallantly. "Hey there, chauffeur, stop this new car of mine at the Shoppy."

As the rusty car drew up Mrs. Tubbs and Mother looked rather agitatedly at a group of young people, girls in smocks and men in white flannels, who were making society noises before the brown barn which had been turned into a tea-room. The two old women felt that they weren't quite dressed for a party; they were shy of silken youth. Mrs. Tubbs's daughter was conscious of the fact that her $1.98 wash-dress, shapeless from many washings, was soiled in front. But Uncle Joe, the old hardshell, was never abashed at anything. He shifted his tobacco quid and "guessed he'd have to get some white pants like that young red-headed fellow's."

Then Father again proved himself magnificent. Wasn't he a New-Yorker? "No flossy tea-room and no bunch of young fellows in ice-cream breeches—probably they were only clerks, anyway, if the truth was known!—was going to scare your Uncle Dudley offn tea! Not that he cared so much for tea itself; 'drather have a good cup of coffee, any time; but he didn't want Joe Tubbs to think he wasn't used to fashionable folks." So, with a manner of wearing goggles and gauntlets, he led the women and the shambling son-in-law and the brazenly sloppy Uncle Joe through the flowery youth and into the raftered room, with its new fireplace and old William and Mary chairs, its highboy covered with brassware, and its little tea-tables with slender handicraft vases each containing one marigold. Father ignored all these elegances and commanded a disdainful waitress with a frilly white apron, "Let's have a couple of tables together here, eh?" He himself shifted chairs, and made a joke, and started to select impressive food.

He was used to New York restaurants, and to quite expensive hotels, for at least once a year, on his birthday, Mr. Pilkings took him to lunch at the Waldorf. While he had apparently been devoting himself to arranging the tables his cunning old brain had determined to order tea and French pastry. Apparently the Tea Shoppe was neutral. There was no French pastry on the bill, but, instead, such curious edibles as cinnamon toast, cream cheese, walnut sandwiches, Martha Washington muffins. Nor was the tea problem so easy as it had seemed. To Father there were only two kinds of tea—the kind you got for a nickel at the Automat, and the kind that Mother privately consumed. But here he had to choose intelligently among orange pekoe, oolong, Ceylon, and English-breakfast teas.

Father did a very brave thing, though he probably will never get the Carnegie medal for it. Instead of timidly asking the lofty waitress's advice, he boldly plunged in and ordered two kinds of sandwiches, cinnamon toast, and, because he liked the name, orange pekoe. He rather held his breath, but apparently the waitress took him quite seriously, and some time in the course of the afternoon actually brought him what he had asked for.

Ye Tea Shoppe was artistic. You could tell that by the fact that none of the arts and crafts wares exposed for sale were in the least useful. And it was too artistic, too far above the sordidness of commercialism, to put any prices on the menu-cards. Consequently Father was worried about his bill all the time he was encouraging his guests to forget their uncomfortably decorative surroundings and talk like regular people. But when he saw how skinny were the sandwiches and how reticent the cinnamon toast he was cheered. He calculated that the whole bill couldn't, in decency, be more than ninety cents for the six of them.

In the midst of his nicest flow of fancy about Mother's fear of mice, the bill was laid decorously on its face beside him. Still talking, but hesitating somewhat, he took a peep at the bill. It was for three dollars and sixty cents.

He felt congealed, but he talked on. He slid a five-dollar bill from his diminutive roll and gallantly paid up. His only comment when, in the car, Mother secretly asked how much he had been overcharged, was the reflection, "They certainly ought to make money out of those tea-rooms. Their profit must be something like five hundred per cent. That strikes me as a pretty good way to earn a living, old lady. You live in a nice comfortable place in the country and don't have to do any work but slice bread and stick in chicken or cream cheese, and make five hundred per cent. Say—"

IV

He didn't say it. But Father had been knocked breathless by an idea. He was silent all the way home. He made figures on the last leaf of his little pocket account-book. He manoeuvered to get Mother alone, and exultantly shot his idea at her.

They were beginning to get old; the city was almost too much for them. They would pick out some pretty, rustic spot and invest their savings in a tea-room. At five-hundred per cent. they would make enough during three months of summer to keep them the rest of the year. If they were located on Cape Cod, perhaps they could spend the winter with the Tubbses. They would have a garden; they would keep chickens, dogs, pussies, yes, a cow; they would buy land, acre by acre; they would have a farm to sustain them when they were too old for work; maybe they would open a whole chain of tea-rooms and ride about supervising them in a motor-car big as a house; they would—

"Now hold your horses, Father," she begged, dizzily. "I never did see such a man for running on. You go on like a house afire. You ought to know more, at your time of life, than to go counting your chickens before—"

"I'm going to hatch them. Don't they tell us in every newspaper and magazine you can lay your hand on that this is the Age of the Man with the Idea? Look here. Two slices of home-made bread, I calc'late, don't cost more than three-fifths of a cent, I shouldn't think, and cream cheese to smear on them about half a cent; there's a little over a cent; and overhead—'course *you* wouldn't take overhead into account, and then you go and say I ain't practical and hatching chickens, and all, but let me tell you, Sarah Jane Appleby, I'm a business man and I've been trained, and I tell you as Pilkings has often said to me, it's overhead that makes or breaks a business, that's what it is, just like he says, yes, sir, *overhead*! So say we'll allow—now let me see, ten plus ten is twenty, and one six-hundredth of twenty would be—six in two is—no, two in six is—well, *anyway*, to make it ab-so-lute-ly safe, we'll allow a cent and a half for each sandwich, to cover overhead and rent and fuel, and then they sell a sandwich at fifteen cents, which is, uh, the way they figure percentage of profit—well, make it, say, seven hundred per cent.! 'Course just estimating roughly like. Now can you beat that? And tea-rooms is a safe, sound, interesting, genteel business if there ever was one. What have you got to say to that?"

Father didn't often thus deluge her with words, but then he didn't often have a Revolutionary Idea. She had never heard of "overhead," and she was impressed; though in some dim confused way she rather associated "overhead" with the rafters of the tea-room. She emerged gasping from the shower, and all she could say was: "Yes: it would be very genteel. And I must say I always did like them hand-painted artistic things. But do you really think it would be safe, Father?"

"Safe? Pooh! Safe's the bank!"

They were in for it. Of course they were going to discuss it back and forth for months, and sit up nights to make figures on the backs of laundry-bills. But they had been fated the moment Father had seen Mother and himself as delightful hosts playing with people in silk sweaters, in a general atmosphere of roses, fresh lobster, and gentility.

They explored the Cape for miles around, looking for a place where they might open a tea-room if they did decide to do so. They said good-by to the Tubbses and returned to New York, to the noisy streets and the thankless drudgery at Pilkings & Son's.

In December they definitely made up their minds to give up the shoe business, take their few hundred dollars from the bank, and, the coming summer, open a tea-room in an old farm-house on the Cliffs at Grimsby Head, Cape Cod.

Out of saving money for the tea-room, that winter, the Applebys had as much fun as they had ever found in spending. They were comrades, partners in getting along without things as they had been partners in working to acquire little luxuries. They went to the movies only once a month—that made the movies only the more thrilling! On the morning before they were to go Father would pound softly on the pillow by Mother's head and sing, "Wake up! It's a fine day and we're going to see a photoplay to-night!"

Mother did without her chocolate peppermints, and Father cut his smoking down to one cigarette after each meal—though occasionally, being but a mortal man, he would fall into sinful ways and smoke up three or four cigarettes while engaged in an enthralling conversation regarding Mr. Pilkings's meanness with fellow-clerks at lunch at the Automat. Afterward he would be very repentant; he would have a severe case of conviction of sin, and Mother would have to comfort him when he accused himself:

"Seems as if I couldn't doggone never learn to control myself. I ain't hopeless, am I? I declare, I'm disgusted with myself when I think of your going without your chocolates and me just making a profane old razorback hog of myself."

There was no sordidness in their minute economy; no chill of poverty; they were saving for an excursion to paradise. They crowed as they thought of the beauty of their discovery: lonely Grimsby Head, where the sea stretched out on one side of their house and moors on the other, with the State road and its motorists only two hundred feet from their door. Though they should live in that sentinel house for years, never would they enjoy it more than they now did in anticipation when they sat of an evening in their brown flat, looking down on a delicatessen, a laundry, and a barber-shop, and planned to invest in their house of accomplished dreams the nickels they were managing to save.

The only thing that worried Father was the fact that their project put upon Mother so great a burden in the way of preparations. At first he took it for granted that only women could know about tea and tea-cups, decorations and paper napkins and art and the disposal of garbage. He determined to learn. By dint of much deep ratiocination while riding in the Elevated between flat and store he evolved the new idea—cheapness.

It was nonsense, he decided, to have egg-shell china and to charge fifteen cents for tea. Why not have neat, inexpensive china, good but not exorbitant tea, and charge only five or ten cents, as did the numerous luncheon-places he knew? Mother eagerly agreed.

Then the man of ideas began to turn his brain to saving Mother the trouble of selecting the tea-room equipment. It was not an easy problem for him. This gallant traveler, who wore his cap so cockily and paid a three-dollar-and-sixty-cent check so nonchalantly when he was traveling, was really an underpaid clerk.

He began by informing himself on all the technicalities of tea-rooms. He lunched at tea-rooms. He prowled in front of tea-rooms. He dreamed about tea-rooms. He became a dabster at tucking paper napkins into his neat little waistcoat without tearing them. He got acquainted with the waitress at the Nickleby Tavern, which was not a tavern, though it was consciously, painstakingly, seriously quaint; and he cautiously made inquiry of her regarding tea and china. During his lunch-hours he frequented auction sales on Sixth Avenue, and became so sophisticated in the matter of second-hand goods that the youngest clerk at Pilkings & Son's, a child of forty who was about to be married, respectfully asked Father about furnishing a flat. He rampaged through department stores without buying a thing, till store detectives secretly followed him. He read the bargain-sale advertisements in his morning paper before he even looked at the war-news head-lines.

Father was no fool, but he had been known to prefer kindliness to convenience. When he could get things for the same price he liked to buy them from small struggling dealers rather than from large and efficient ones—thereby, in his innocent way, helping to perpetuate the old system of weak, unskilled, casual, chaotically competitive businesses. This kindliness moved him when, during his search for information about tea-room accessories, he encountered a feeble but pretentious racket-store which a young Hungarian had established on Twenty-sixth Street, just off Sixth Avenue. The Hungarian and one girl assistant were trying by futile garish window-decorations to draw trade from the great department stores and the five-and-ten-cent stores on one side of them and the smart shops on the other side. But the Hungarian was clever, too clever. He first found out all of Father's plans, then won Father's sympathy. He coughed a little, and with a touching smile which was intended to rouse admiration, declared that his lungs were bad, but never mind, he would fight on, and go away for a rest when he had succeeded. He insinuated that, as he was not busy now, he could do all the buying and get better terms from wholesalers or bankruptcy bargain sales than could Father himself. The Hungarian's best stock in trading with Father was to look young and pathetically threadbare, to smile and shake his head and say playfully, as though he were trying to hide his secret generosity by a pretense of severity, "But of course I'd charge you a commission—you see I'm a hard-hearted fella."

It was January. In a month, now, Mother would be grunting heavily and beginning the labor of buying for the tea-room. So far she had done nothing but crochet two or three million tidies for the tea-room chairs, "to make them look homey."

The Hungarian showed Father tea-cups with huge quantities of gold on them. He assured Father that it was smarter to buy odd cups—also cheaper, as thus they could take advantage of broken lots and closing-out sales. Fascinated, Father kept hanging around, and at last he bolted frantically and authorized the Hungarian to purchase everything for him.

Which the Hungarian had already done, knowing that the fly was on the edge of the web.

You know, the things didn't look so bad, not so very bad—as long as they were new.

Tea-cups and saucers gilded like shaving-mugs and equally thick. Golden-oak chairs of mid-Chautauquan patterns, with backs of saw-mill Heppelwhite; chairs of cane and rattan with fussy scrolls and curlicues of wicker, the backs set askew. Reed tables with gollops of wicker; plain black wooden tables that were like kitchen tables once removed; folding-tables that may have been suitable to card-playing, if you didn't play anything more exciting than casino. Flat silver that was heavily plated except where it was likely to wear. Tea-pots of mottled glaze, and cream-jugs with knobs of gilt, and square china ash-trays on which one instinctively expected to find the legend "Souvenir of Niagara Falls." Too many cake-baskets and too few sugar-bowls. Dark blue plates with warts on the edges and melancholy landscapes painted in the centers. Chintzes and wall-papers of patterns fashionable in 1890. Tea-cartons that had the most inspiring labels; cocoa that was bitter and pepper that was mild; preserves that were generous with hayseed and glucose.

But everything was varnished that could be varnished; everything was tied with pink ribbon that would stand for it; the whole collection looked impressively new to a man accustomed to a shabby flat; the prices seemed reasonable; and Mother was saved practically all the labor of buying.

She had clucked comfortably every time he had worried aloud about her task. Yet she was secretly troubled. It gave her a headache to climb down the four flights of stairs from their flat. The acrid dust of the city streets stung her eyes, the dissonant grumble of a million hurrying noises dizzied her, and she would stand on a street-corner for five minutes before daring to cross. When Father told her that all the buying was done, and awaiting her approval, she gasped. But she went down with him, was impressed by the shininess and newness of things—and the Hungarian was given a good share of the Applebys' life-savings, agitatedly taken out of the savings-bank in specie.

They had purchased freedom. The house at Grimsby Head was eager for them. Mother cried as she ripped up the carpet in their familiar flat and saw the treasured furniture rudely crated for shipment to the unknown. She felt that she was giving up ever so many metropolitan advantages by leaving New York so prematurely. Why, she'd never been inside Grant's Tomb! She'd miss her second cousin—not that she'd seen the cousin for a year or two. And on the desert moors of Grimsby she couldn't run across the street to a delicatessen. But none of the inconveniences of going away so weighed upon her spirit as did the memory of their hours together in this flat.

But when she stood with him on the steamer again, bound for the Cape, when the spring breeze gave life to her faded hair, she straightened her shoulders and stood like a conqueror.

"Gee! we'll be at Grimsby to-morrow," piped Father, throwing his coat open and debonairly sticking his thumbs into his lower waistcoat pockets. "The easy life for me, old lady. I'm going to sit in a chair in the sun and watch you work."

"How you do run on!" she said. "You wait and find out the way you have to wash dishes and all. We'll see what we see, my fine young whiffet."

"Say, James J. Jerusalem but I've got a fine idea. I know what we'll call the tea-room—'The T Room'—see, not spelling out the T. Great, eh?"

V

It was May in Arcady, and those young-hearted old lovers, Mr. and Mrs. Seth Appleby, were almost ready to open the tea-room. They had leased for a term of two years an ancient and weathered house on the gravel cliffs of Grimsby Head. From the cliffs the ocean seemed more sweepingly vast than when beheld from the beach, and the plain of it was colored like a pearly shell. To the other side of their dream-house were moors that might have been transplanted from Devon, rolling uplands covered with wiry grass that was springy to the feet, dappled with lichens which gave to the spacious land its lovely splashes of color—rose and green and sulphur and quiet gray.

It was a lonely countryside; the nearest signs of human life were a church gauntly silhouetted on the hill above Grimsby Center, two miles away, and a life-saving station, squat and sand-colored, slapped down in a hollow of the cliffs. But near the Applebys' door ran the State road, black and oily and smooth, on which, even at the beginning of the summer season, passed a procession of motors from Boston and Brockton, Newport and New York, all of them unquestionably filled with people who would surely discover that they were famished for tea and preserves and tremendous quantities of sandwiches, as soon as Father and Mother hung out the sign, "The T Room."

They would open in a day or two, now, when Mother had finished the livid chintz window-curtains. The service-room was already crammed with chairs and tables till it resembled a furniture-store. A maid was established, a Cape Verde Portygee girl from Mashpee. All day long Father had been copying the menu upon the florid cards which he had bought from a bankrupt Jersey City printer—thick gilt-edged cards embossed with forget-me-nots in colors which hadn't quite registered.

From their upper rooms, in which Mother had arranged the furniture to make the new home resemble their New York flat, the Applebys came happily down-stairs for the sunset. They were still excited at having country and sea at their door; still felt that all life would be one perpetual vacation. Every day now they would have the wild peace of the Cape, for two weeks of which, each year, they had had to work fifty weeks. Think of stepping out to a view of the sea instead of a view of Brambach's laundry! They were, in fact, as glad to get into the open as the city-seeking youngster is to get away from it.

On the landward side of the bleak house, crimson-rambler roses were luxuriant, and a stiff shell-bordered garden gave charily of small marigolds. Riches were these, by comparison with the two geraniums in a window-box which had been their New York garden. But they had an even greater pride—the rose-arbor. Sheltered by laurel from the sea winds was a whitewashed lattice, covered with crimson ramblers. Through a gap in the laurels they could see the ocean, stabbingly blue in contrast to the white dunes which reared battlements along the top of the gravel cliff. Far out a coasting schooner blossomed on the blue skyline. Bees hummed and the heart was quiet. Already the Applebys had found the place of brooding blossoms for which they had hoped; already they loved the rose-arbor as they had never loved the city. He nuzzled her cheek like an old horse out at pasture, and "Old honey!" he whispered.

Two days more, and they had the tea-room ready for its opening.

Father insisted on giving the evening over to wild ceremonies. He played "Juanita" and "Kelly with the Green Necktie," and other suitable chants upon that stately instrument, the mouth-organ, and marched through the tea-room banging on a dishpan with the wooden salad-spoon. Suddenly he turned into the first customer, and seating himself in a lordly manner, with his legs crossed, his thumbs in his waistcoat pockets and his hands waving fan-wise, he ordered, "Lettuce sandwiches, sody-water, a tenderloin steak, fish-balls, a bottle of champagne, and ice-cream with beef gravy, and hustle my order, young woman."

Mother was usually too shy for make-believe, but this time she was stirred to stand with her fat doll-arms akimbo, and to retort, "You'll get nothing here, young fellow. This is a place for ladies and gents only!"

They squealed and hugged each other. From the kitchen door the Portygee maid viewed her employers with lofty scorn, as Father gave a whole series of imitations of the possible first customer, who, as variously presented, might be Jess Willard, Senator Lodge, General von Hindenburg, or Mary Pickford.

At four next afternoon, with the solemn trembling of an explorer hoisting the flag to take possession of new territory, they hung out their sign, stepped back to admire it as it swung and shone against the crimson ramblers, and watched for the next motor-car.

It was coming! It was a seven-passenger car, filled with women in blanket coats. One of them actually waved, as the car approached the little couple who were standing in the sun, unconsciously arm in arm. Then the car had streaked by, was gone round the bend.

The second car passed them, and the third. A long intense period when the road was vacant. Then the fourth and fifth cars, almost together; and the file of motorists turned from exciting prospects into just motorists, passing strangers, oblivious of the two old people under their hopeful sign.

While they were forlornly re-entering the house the eleventh car suddenly stopped, and five hungry people trooped into the tea-room with demands for tea and muffins and cake. The Applebys didn't have muffins, but they did have sandwiches, and everybody was happy. Mother shooed the maid out into the kitchen, and herself, with awkward eagerness to get orders exactly right, leaned over the tea-table. In the kitchen Father stuffed kindling into the stove to bring the water to a boil again, and pantingly seized the bread-knife and attacked a loaf as though he were going to do it a violence. Mother entered, took the knife away from him, and dramatically drove him out to cut up more kindling.

The customers were served. While they ate and drank, and talked about what they had eaten and drunk at lunch at an inn, they were unconscious of two old pairs of eyes that watched them from the kitchen door, as brightly, as furtively, as excitedly as two birds in a secret thicket. The host paid without remarks what seemed to the Applebys an enormous bill, a dollar and sixty cents, and rambled out to the car, still unknowing that two happy people wanted to follow him with their blessings. This history is unable to give any further data regarding him; when his car went round the bend he disappeared from the fortunes of the Applebys, and he was not to know how much blessing he had scattered. I say, perhaps he was you who read this—you didn't by any chance happen to be motoring between Yarmouth and Truro, May 16, 1915, did you? With five in the party; coffee-colored car with one mud-guard slightly twisted?

The season was not quick in opening. To the Applebys the time between mid-May and mid-June was crawlingly slow. On some days they had two orders; some days, none at all. Of an evening, before they could sink into the sunset-colored peace of the rose-arbor, they had to convince themselves that they couldn't really expect any business till the summerites had begun to take their vacations. There was a curious psychological fact. It had always been Father, the brisk burden-bearer, who had comforted the secluded Mother. He had brought back to the flat the strenuousness of business. But inactivity was hard on his merry heart; he fretted and fussed at having nothing to do; he raged at having to throw away unused bread because it was growing stale. It was Mother who reminded him that they couldn't expect business before the season.

Mid-June came; the stream of cars was almost a solid parade; the Portygee maid brought the news that there were summer boarders at the Nickerson farm-house; and the Applebys, when they were in Grimsby Center buying butter and bread, saw the rocking-chair brigade mobilizing on the long white porches of the Old Harbor Inn.

And trade began!

There was no rival tea-room within ten miles. Father realized with a thumping heart that he had indeed chosen well in selecting Grimsby Head. Ten, twelve, even fifteen orders a day came from the motorists. The chronic summerites, they who came to Grimsby Center each year, walked over to see the new tea-room and to purchase Mother's home-made doughnuts. On June 27th the Applebys made a profit of $4.67, net.

As they rested in the rose-arbor at dusk of that day, Father burst out in desperate seriousness: "Oh my dear, my dear, it is going to go! I was beginning to get scared. I couldn't have forgiven myself if I'd let you in for something that would have been a failure. Golly! I've been realizing that we would have been pretty badly up against it if the tea-room hadn't panned out right. I'd have wanted to shoot myself if I'd been and gone and led you into want, old honey!"

Then, after the first of July, when the Cape Cod season really began, business suddenly fell away to nothing. They couldn't understand it. In panic they reduced the price of tea to five cents. No result. They had about one customer a day. They had not looked to Grimsby Center for the cause. That they might personally attend to business they had been sending the maid to the Center for their supplies, while they stuck at home—and wore out their hearts in vain hoping, in terrified wonder as to why the invisible gods had thus smitten them. Not for a week, a week of draining expense without any income to speak of, did they find out.

One July evening they walked to Grimsby Center. Half-way down they came to a new sign, shaped like a tea-pot, declaring in a striking block of print:

Miss Mitchin Of Brookline Announces The Quaintest Tea-Room On The Cape. Historic Soule Mansion,

GRIMSBY CENTER. CRUMPETS AND SALLY LUNNS WITH
FRESH STRAWBERRY JAM. OPEN JULY 1.

And the Applebys had never heard of crumpets or Sally Lunns.

While the light turned the moors to a wistful lavender, the little old
couple stood in a hollow of the road, looking mutely up at the sign that
mocked them from its elevation on a bare gravel bank beside the way.
Father's shoulders braced; he bit his lips; he reached out for Mother's
hand and patted it. He led her on, and it was he who spoke first:

"Oh, that kind of miffle-business won't hurt us any. Girly-girly stuff,
that's what it is. Regular autoists would rather have one of your home-
made doughnuts than all the crumples in the world, and you can just
bet your bottom dollar on that, Sary Jane."

He even chuckled, but it was a feeble chuckle, and he could find
no other solace to give as they trudged toward Grimsby Center, two
insignificant people, hand in hand, dim in the melancholy light which
made mysterious the stretching moors. Presently they and the black
highroad disappeared. Only the sandy casual trails and mirror-bright
tiny pools stood out in the twilight.

Yet there was light enough for them to see the silhouettes of two
more tea-pot signs before they entered Grimsby Center.

The village was gay, comparatively. There was to be a motion-picture
show in the town hall, and the sign advertising it was glaring with no
less than four incandescent lights. In the Old Harbor Inn the guests
were dancing to phonograph music, after their early supper. A man
who probably meant well was playing long, yellowish, twilit wails on
a cornet, somewhere on the outskirts. Girls in sailor jumpers, with
vivid V's of warmly tanned flesh, or in sweaters of green and rose and
violet and canary yellow, wandered down to the post-office. To the
city-bred Applebys there would have been cheer and excitement in this
mild activity, after their farm-house weeks; indeed Father suggested,
"We ought to stay and see the movies. Look! Royal X. Snivvles in 'The
Lure of the Crimson Cobra'—six reels—that sounds snappy." But his
exuberance died in a sigh. A block down Harpoon Street they saw a sign,
light-encircled, tea-pot shaped, hung out from a great elm. Without
explanations they turned toward it.

They passed a mansion of those proud old days when whalers and
China traders and West-Indiamen brought home gold and blacks,
Cashmere shawls and sweet sandalwood, Malay oaths and the jawbones

of whales. The Applebys could see by the electric lights bowered in the lilac-bushes that a stately grass walk, lined with Madonna lilies and hollyhock and phlox, led to the fanlight-crested white door, above which hung the mocking tea-pot sign. The house was lighted, the windows open. To the right of the hall was the arts-shop where, among walls softened with silky Turkish rugs and paintings of blue dawn amid the dunes, were tables of black-and-white china, sports hats, and Swiss toys, which the Grimsby summer colony meekly bought at the suggestion of the sprightly Miss Mitchin.

To the left was the dining-room, full of small white candle-lighted tables and the sound of laughter.

"Gosh! they even serve supper there!" Father's voice complained. He scarcely knew that he had spoken. Like Mother, he was picturing their own small tea-room and the cardboard-shaded oil-lamp that lighted it.

"Come, don't let's stand here," said Mother, fiercely, and they trailed forlornly past. They were not so much envious as in awe of Miss Mitchin's; it seemed to belong to the same unattainable world as Newport and the giant New York hotels.

The Applebys didn't know it, but Grimsby Center had become artistic. They couldn't know it, but that sharp-nosed genius-hound Miss Mitchin was cashing in on her *salon*. She came from Brookline, hence Massachusetts Brahmins of almost pure caste could permit themselves to be seen at her tea-room. But nowadays she spent her winters in New York, as an artistic photographer, and she entertained interior decorators, minor fiction-writers, and minus poets with free food every Thursday evening. It may be hard to believe, but in A.D. 1915 she was still calling her grab-bag of talent a "*salon*." It was really a saloon, with a literary free-lunch counter. In return, whenever they could borrow the price from commercialized friends, the yearners had her take their photographs artistically, which meant throwing the camera out of focus and producing masterpieces which were everything except likenesses.

When Miss Mitchin resolved to come to Grimsby Center her group of writers, who had protected themselves against the rude, crude world of business men and lawyers by living together in Chelsea Village, were left defenseless. They were in danger of becoming human. So they all followed Miss Mitchin to Grimsby, and contentedly went on writing about one another.

There are many such groups, with the same summer watering-places and the same winter beering-places. Some of them drink hard liquor and play cards. But Miss Mitchin's group were very mild in manner, though desperately violent in theory. The young women wore platter-sized tortoise-shell spectacles and smocks that were home-dyed to a pleasing shrimp pink. The young men also wore tortoise-shell spectacles, but not smocks—not usually, at least. One of them had an Albanian costume and a beard that was a cross between the beard of an early Christian martyr on a diet and that of a hobo who merely needed a shave. Elderly ladies loved to have him one-step with them and squeeze their elbows.

All of the yearners read their poetry aloud, very superior, and rising in the inflections. It is probable that they made a living by taking in one another's literary washing. But they were ever so brave about their financial misfortunes, and they could talk about the ballet Russe and also charlotte russes in quite the nicest way. Indeed it was a pretty sight to see them playing there on the lawn before the Mitchin mansion, talking about the novels they were going to write and the revolutions they were going to lead.

Had Miss Mitchin's ballet of hobohemians been tough newspapermen they wouldn't have been drawing-cards for a tea-room. But these literary ewe-lambs were a spectacle to charm the languishing eyes of the spinsters who filled the Old Harbor Inn and the club-women from the yellow water regions who were viewing the marvels of nature as displayed on and adjacent to the ocean. Practically without exception these ladies put vine leaves in their hair—geranium leaves, anyway—and galloped to Miss Mitchin's, to drink tea and discuss Freud and dance the fox-trot in a wild, free, artistic, somewhat unstandardized manner.

Because it was talked about and crowded, ordinary untutored motorists judged Miss Mitchin's the best place to go, and permitted their wives to drag them past the tortoise-shell spectacles and the unprostituted art and the angular young ladies in baggy smocks breaking out in sudden irresponsible imitations of Pavlova.

None of this subtlety, this psycho-analysis and fellowship of the arts, was evident to the Applebys. They didn't understand the problem, "Why is a Miss Mitchin?" All that they knew, as they dragged weary joints down the elm-rustling road and back to the bakery on Main Street, was that Miss Mitchin's caravanserai was intimidatingly grand—and very busy.

They were plodding out of town again when Mother exclaimed, "Why, Father, you forgot to get your cigarettes."

"No, I—Oh, I been smoking too much. Do me good to lay off."

They had gone half a mile farther before she sighed: "Cigarettes don't cost much. 'Twouldn't have hurt you to got 'em. You get 'em the very next time we're in town—or send Katie down. I won't have you denying—"

Her voice droned away. They could think of nothing but mean economies as they trudged the wide and magic night of the moors.

When they were home, and the familiar golden-oak chairs and tidies blurred their memory of Miss Mitchin's crushing competition, Father again declared that no dinky tea-pot inn could permanently rival Mother's home-made doughnuts. But he said it faintly then, and more faintly on the days following, for inactivity again enervated him—made him, for the first time in his life, feel almost old.

VI

Apparently the Applebys' customers had liked "The T Room" well enough—some of them had complimented Mrs. Appleby on the crispness of her doughnuts, the generousness of her chicken sandwiches. Those who had quarreled about the thickness of the bread or the vagueness of flavor in the tea Father had considered insulting, and he had been perky as a fighting-sparrow in answering them. A good many must have been pleased, for on their trip back from Provincetown they returned, exclaimed that they remembered the view from the rose-arbor, and chatted with Father about the roads and New York and fish. As soon as the first novelty of Miss Mitchin's was gone, the Applebys settled down to custom which was just large enough to keep their hopes staggering onward, and just small enough to eat away their capital a few cents a day, instead of giving them a profit.

In the last week of July they were visited by their daughter Lulu—Lulu the fair, Lulu the spectacled, Lulu the lily wife of Harris Hartwig, the up-to-date druggist of Saserkopee, New York.

Lulu had informed them two weeks beforehand that they were to be honored with the presence of herself and her son Harry; and Father and Mother had been unable to think of any excuse strong enough to keep her away. Lulu wasn't unkind to her parents; rather, she was too kind; she gave them good advice and tried to arrange Mother's hair in the coiffures displayed by Mrs. Edward Schuyler Deflaver of Saserkopee, who gave smart teas at the Woman's Exchange. Lulu cheerily told Father how well he was withstanding the hand of Time, which made him feel decrepit and become profane.

In fact, though they took it for granted that they adored their dear daughter Lulu, they knew that they would not enjoy a single game of cribbage, nor a single recital by Signor Sethico Applebi the mouth-organ virtuoso, as long as she was with them. But she was coming, and Mother frantically cleaned everything and hid her favorite old shoes.

Mrs. Lulu Hartwig arrived with a steamer-trunk, two new gowns, a camera, and Harry. She seemed disappointed not to find a large summer hotel with dancing and golf next door to "The T Room," and she didn't hesitate to say that her parents would have done better—which meant that Lulu would have enjoyed her visit more—if they had "located" at Bar Harbor or Newport. She rearranged the furniture, but as there was nothing in the tea-room but chairs, tables, and a fireplace, there wasn't much she could do.

She descended on Grimsby Center, and came back enthusiastic about Miss Mitchin's. She had met the young man with the Albanian costume, and he had talked to her about vorticism and this jolly new Polish composer with his suite for tom-tom and cymbals. She led Father into the arbor and effervescently demanded, "Why don't Mother and you have a place like that dear old mansion of Miss Mitchin's, and all those clever people there and all?"

Father fairly snarled, "Now look here, young woman, the less you say about Miss Mitten the more popular you'll be around here. And don't you dare to speak to your mother about that place. It's raised the devil with our trade, and I won't have your mother bothered with it. And if you mean the young fellow that needs a decent pair of pantaloons by this 'Albanian costume' business, why I sh'd think you'd be ashamed to speak of him."

"Now, Father, of course you have particularly studied artists—"

"Look here, young woman, when you used to visit us in New York, it was all right for you to get our goats by sticking your snub nose in the air and asking us if we'd read a lot of new-fangled books that we'd never heard of. I'll admit that was a good way to show us how superior you were. But this Miss Mitten place is a pretty serious proposition for us to buck, and I absolutely forbid you to bother your mother with mentioning it."

Father stood straight and glared at her. There was in him nothing of the weary little man who was in awe of Miss Mitchin's. Even his daughter was impressed. She forgot for a moment that she was Mrs. Hartwig, now, and had the best phonograph in Saserkopee. But she took one more shot:

"All the same, it would be a good thing for you if you had some clever people—or some society people—coming here often. It would advertise the place as nothing else would."

"Well, we'll see about that," said Father—which meant, of course, that he wouldn't see about it.

Lulu Hartwig was a source of agitation for two weeks. After Father's outbreak she stopped commenting, but every day when business was light they could feel her accusingly counting the number of customers. But she did not become active again till the Sunday before her going.

The Applebys were sitting up-stairs, that day, holding hands and avoiding Lulu. Below them they heard a motor-car stop, and Mother prepared to go down and serve the tourists. The brazen, beloved voice of Uncle Joe Tubbs of West Skipsit blared out: "Where's the folks, heh? Tell 'em the Tubbses are here."

And Lulu's congealed voice, in answer: "I don't know whether they are at home. If they are, who shall I tell them is calling, please?"

"Huh? Oh, well, just say the Tubbses."

"Mr. and Mrs. Tubbs?"

"Yes, yes, yes, yes, yes!"

By this time Father and Mother were galloping down-stairs. They welcomed the Tubbses with yelps of pleasure; the four of them sat in rockers on the grass and talked about the Tubbses' boarders, and the Applebys admired to hear that Uncle Joe now ran the car himself. But all of them were conscious that Lulu, in a chiffon scarf and eye-glasses, was watching them amusedly, and the Tubbses uneasily took leave in an hour, pleading the distance back to West Skipsit.

Not till evening, when he got the chance to walk by himself on the beach below the gravel cliffs, did Father quite realize what his daughter had done—that, with her superior manner, she had frightened the Tubbses away. Yet there was nothing to do about it.

Even at her departure there was a certain difficulty, for Lulu developed a resolution to have her parents visit her at Saserkopee. Perhaps she wished to show them in what state she now lived; or it may conceivably be that, in her refined and determined manner, she was fond of her parents. She kissed them repeatedly and was gone with much waving of a handkerchief and yelps of "Now don't forget—you're you're to visit me—be sure and write—Harry, don't stick your head out of the window, d'yuhhearme?"

LULU'S VISIT HAD TWO EFFECTS upon the lives of Father and Mother. They found that their quiet love had grown many-fold stronger, sweeter, in the two weeks it had been denied the silly fondnesses of utterance. They could laugh, now that there was no critic of their shy brand of humor. Father stopped on the step and winked an immense shameless wink at Mother, and she sighed and said, with unexpected understanding, "Yes, I'm afraid Lulu is a little—just a leet-le bit—"

"And I reckon we won't be in such a gosh-awful hustle to visit her."

Mother was so vulgar as to grunt, "Well, I guess not!"

That evening they sat in the rose-arbor again. And had tone poems on the mouth-organ. And dreamed that something would happen to make their investment pay.

Another result there was of Lulu's visit. Father couldn't help remembering her suggestion that they ought to bag a social or artistic lion as an attraction for "The T Room." He was delighted to find that, after weeks of vacuous worry, he had another idea.

Now that August, the height of the season, had come, he would capture Mrs. Vance Carter herself.

Mrs. Vance Carter was the widow of the Boothbay Textile Mills millions. She was a Winslow on her father's side, a Cabot on her mother's, and Beacon Street was officially swept from end to end and tidied with little pink feather dusters whenever she returned to Boston. She was so solid that society reporters didn't dare write little items about her, and when she was in Charleston she was invited to the Saint Cecilia Ball. Also she was rather ignorant, rather unhappy, and completely aimless. She and her daughter spent their summers three miles from Grimsby Head, in an estate with a gate-house and a conservatory and a golf course and a house with three towers and other architecture. When America becomes a military autocracy she will be Lady Carter or the Countess of Grimsby.

The Applebys saw her go by every day, in a landaulet with liveried chauffeur and footman.

With breathless secrecy Father planned to entice Mrs. Vance Carter to "The T Room." Once they had her there, she would certainly appreciate the wholesome goodness of Mother's cooking. He imagined long intimate conversations in which Mrs. Carter would say to him, "Mr. Appleby, I can't tell you how much I like to get away from my French cook and enjoy your nice old house and Mrs. Appleby's delicious homey doughnuts." It was easy to win Mrs. Carter, in imagination. Sitting by himself in the rose-arbor while Mother served their infrequent customers or stood at the door unhappily watching for them, Father visualized Mrs. Carter exclaiming over the view from the arbor, the sunset across the moors as seen from their door—which was, Father believed, absolutely the largest and finest sunset in the world. He even went so far as to discover in Mrs. Vance Carter, Mrs. Cabot-Winslow-Carter, a sneaking fondness for cribbage, which, in her exalted social position, she had had to conceal. He saw her send the chauffeur away, and cache her lorgnette, and roll up her sleeves, and simply wade into an orgy of cribbage, with pleasing light refreshments of cider and cakes waiting by the fireplace. Then he saw Mrs. Carter sending all her acquaintances to "The T Room," and the establishment so prosperous that Miss Mitchin would come around and beg the Applebys to enter into partnership.

Father was not such a fool as to believe all his fancies. But hadn't he heard the most surprising tales of how friendly these great folk could be? Why here just the other day he had been reading in the boiler-plate innards of the *Grimsby Recorder* how Jim Hill, the railroad king, had dropped off at a little station in North Dakota one night, incog., and talked for hours to the young station-master.

He was burning to do something besides helping Mother in the kitchen—something which would save them and pull the tea-room out of the hole. Without a word to Mother he started for Grimsby Hill, the estate of Mrs. Vance Carter. He didn't know what he was going to do, but he was certain that he was going to do something.

As he arrived at the long line of iron picket fence surrounding Grimsby Hill, he saw Mrs. Carter's motor enter the gate. It seemed to be a good omen. He hurried to the gate, peered in, then passed on. He couldn't go and swagger past that exclusive-looking gate-house and intrude on that sweep of rhododendron-lined private driveway. He walked shyly along the iron fence for a quarter of a mile before he got up courage to go back, rush through the towering iron gateway and past the gate-house, into the sacred estate. He expected to hear a voice— it would be a cockney servant's voice—demanding, "'Ere you, wot do you want?" But no one stopped him; no one spoke to him; he was safe among the rhododendrons. He clumped along as though he had important business, secretly patting his tie into shape and smoothing his hair. Just let anybody try to stop him! He knew what he was about! But he really didn't know what he was about; he hadn't the slightest notion as to whether he would go up and invite their dear cribbage-companion Mrs. Carter to come and see them or tack up a "T Room" advertisement on the porch.

He came to a stretch of lawn, with the house and all its three towers scowling down at him. Behind it were the edges of a group of out-buildings. He veered around toward these. Outside the garage he saw the chauffeur, with his livery coat off, polishing a fender. Great! Perhaps he could persuade the chauffeur to help him. He put on what he felt to be a New York briskness, furtively touched his tie again, and skipped up to the chauffeur.

"Fine day!" he said, breezily, starting with the one neutral topic of conversation in the world.

"What of it?" said the chauffeur, and went on polishing.

"Well, uh, say, I wanted to have a talk with you."

"I guess there's nothing stopping you. G'wan and have your talk. I can't get away. The old dragon wanted to have a talk with me, too, this morning. So did the housekeeper. Everybody does." And he polished harder than ever.

"Ha, ha!" Which indicates Father's laughter, though actually it sounded more like "Hick, hick!" As carelessly as he could Father observed: "That's how it goes, all right. I know. When I was in the shoe business—"

"Waal, waal, you don't say so, Si! Haow's the shoe business in Hyannis, papa?"

"Hyannis, hell! I've been in business in New York City, New York, for more than forty years!"

"Oh!"

Father felt that he had made an impression. He stuck his thumbs in his waistcoat pockets—as he had not done these six gloomy weeks—threw out his chest, and tried to look like Thirty-fourth and Broadway, with a dash of Wall Street and a flavor of Fifth Avenue.

The chauffeur sighed, "Well, all I can say is that any guy that's lived in New York that long and then comes to this God-forsaken neck of land is a nut."

With an almost cosmic sorrow in his manner and an irritated twist in his suspenders, the chauffeur disappeared into the garage. Father forlornly felt that he wasn't visibly getting nearer to the heart and patronage of Mrs. Vance Carter.

He stood alone on the cement terrace before the garage. The square grim back of the big house didn't so much "look down on him" as beautifully ignore him. A maid in a cap peeped wonderingly at him from a window. A man in dun livery wheeled a vacuum cleaner out of an unexpected basement door. An under-gardener, appearing at the corner, dragging a cultivator, stared at him. Far off, somewhere, he heard a voice crying, "Fif' love!" He could see a corner of a sunken garden with stiff borders of box. He had an uneasy feeling that a whole army of unexpected servants stood between him and Mrs. Vance Carter; that, at any moment, a fat, side-whiskered, expensive butler, like the butlers you see in the movies, would pop up and order him off the grounds.

The unsatisfactory chauffeur reappeared. In a panic Father urged, "Say, my name's Appleby and I run the tea-room at Grimsby Head—

you know, couple of miles this side of the Center. It would be pretty nice for our class of business if the Madam was to stop there some time, and I was just wondering, just kinda wondering, if some time when she felt thirsty you c—"

"She don't never tell me when she's thirsty. She just tells me when she's mad."

"Well, you know, some time you might be stopping to show her the view or something—you fix it up, and—Here, you get yourself some cigars." He timidly held out a two-dollar bill. It seemed to bore the chauffeur a good deal, but he condescended to take it. Father tried to look knowing and friendly and sophisticated all at once. He added, "Any time you feel like a good cup o' tea and the finest home-made doughnuts you ever ate, why, you just drop in yourself, and 'twon't cost you a cent."

"All right, 'bo, I'll see what I can do," said the chauffeur, and vanished again.

Father airily stamped along the driveway. His head was high and hopeful. He inspected the tennis-courts as though he were Maurice McLoughlin. He admitted that the rhododendrons were quite extensive. In fact, he liked Grimsby Hill.

He had saved their fortunes—not for himself, but for Mother. He whistled "The Harum-Scarum Rag" all the way home, interrupting himself only to murmur: "I wonder where the back door of that house is. Not at the back, anyway. Never saw even a garbage-pail."

And then for two weeks he sat with Mother in the sun and watched the motors go by.

They were almost ready to admit, now, that their venture was a complete failure; that they were ruined; that they didn't know what they would do, with no savings and a rainy day coming.

They let their maid go. They gave the grocer smaller and smaller orders for bread and butter and cheese—and even these orders were invariably too large for the little custom that came their way.

For a week Father concealed the fact that Mrs. Vance Carter would be coming—not now, but very soon. Then he had to tell Mother the secret to save her from prostrating worry. They talked always of that coming miracle as they sat with hand desperately clutching hand in the evening; they nearly convinced themselves that Mrs. Carter would send her friends. September was almost here, and it was too late for Mrs. Carter's influence to help them this year, but they trusted that somehow, by the magic of her wealth and position, she would enable them to get through the winter and find success during the next year.

They developed a remarkable skill in seeing her car coming far down the road. When either of them saw it the other was summoned, and they waited tremblingly. But the landaulet always passed, with Mrs. Carter staring straight ahead, gray-haired and hook-nosed; sometimes with Miss Margaret Carter, whose softly piquant little nose would in time be hooked like her mother's. Father's treacherous ally the chauffeur never even looked at "The T Room." Sometimes Father wondered if the chauffeur knew just where the house was; perhaps he had never noticed it. He planned to wave and attract the chauffeur's attention, but in face of the prodigious Mrs. Carter he never dared to carry out the plan.

September 1st. The Applebys had given up hope of miracles. They were making up their minds to notify Mr. Pilkings, of Pilkings & Son's Sixth Avenue Standard Shoe Parlor, that Father again wanted the job he had held for so many years.

They must leave the rose-arbor for the noise of that most alien of places, their native New York.

Mother was in the kitchen; Father at the front door, aimlessly whittling. He looked up, saw the Vance Carter motor approach. He shrugged his shoulders, growled, "Let her go to the dickens."

Then the car had stopped, and Mrs. Vance Carter and Miss Margaret Carter had incredibly stepped out, had started up the path to the tea-room.

VII

Father's hand kept on aimlessly whittling, while his eyes poked out like those of a harassed fiddler-crab when he saw Mrs. Vance Carter actually stop. It was surely a dream. In his worry over inactivity he had found himself falling into queer little illusions lately. He was conscious that the chauffeur, whom he had bribed to stop some day, was winking at him in a vulgar manner not at all appropriate to his dove-gray uniform. He had a spasm of indignant wonder. "I'll bet a hat that fellow didn't have a thing to do with this; he's a grafter." Then he sprang up, bowing.

Mrs. Carter rustled up to him and murmured, "May we have some tea, here, and a cake, do you know?"

"Oh yes, ma'am! Won't you step right in? Fine day, ma'am."

Mrs. Carter seemed not to have any opinions regarding the day. Quite right, too; it wasn't an especially fine day; just *a day*.

She marched in, gave one quick, nervous look, and said, with tremendous politeness: "May we have this table by the window? You have such a charming view over the cliffs."

"Oh yes, ma'am! We hoped some day you'd take that table. Kind of kept the view for you," said Father, with panting gallantry, fairly falling over himself as he rushed across the floor to pull out their chairs and straighten the table-cloth.

Mrs. Carter paid no attention to him whatsoever. She drew a spectacle-case from her small hand-bag and set upon her beetling nose a huge pair of horn-rimmed eye-glasses. She picked up the menu-card as though she were delicately removing a bug—supposing there to be any bug so presumptuous as to crawl upon her smart tan suit. She raised her chin and held the card high.

"Uh, tea, lettuce sandwiches, cream-cheese sandwiches, chicken sandwiches, doughnuts, cinnamon toast," she read off to her daughter.

So quickly that he started, she turned on Father and demanded, "What sort of tea have you, please?"

"Why, uh—just a minute and I'll ask."

Father bolted through the door into the large, clean, woodeny, old-fashioned kitchen, where Mother was wearily taking a batch of doughnuts out of the fat-kettle.

"Mother!" he exulted. "Mrs. Carter—she's here!"

Mother dropped the doughnuts back into the kettle. The splashing fat must have burnt her, but beyond mutely wiping the grease from her hand, she paid no attention to it. She turned paper white. "Oh, Seth!" she groaned. Then, in agony, "After your going and getting them here, I haven't a thing ready for them but lettuce sandwiches and fresh doughnuts."

"Never mind. I'll make them take those. Say, what kind of tea have we got now?"

"Oh, dear! we haven't got a thing left but just—well, it's just tea, mixed."

He galloped back into the tea-room, frightened lest the royal patrons leave before they were served. On the way he resolved to lie—not as the pinching tradesman lies, smugly and unconsciously, but desperately, to save Mother.

"We have orange pekoe and oolong," he gasped.

"Then you might give us some orange pekoe and—oh, two chicken sandwiches."

"Gee! I'm awfully sorry, ma'am, but we're just out of chicken sandwiches. If we'd only known *you* were coming—But we have some very nice fresh lettuce sandwiches, and I do wish you would try some of our doughnuts. They're fresh-made, just this minute."

He clasped his hands, pressed them till the fingers of one gouged the back of the other. Father was not a Uriah Heep. At Pilkings & Son's he had often "talked back" to some of his best customers. But now he would gladly have licked Mrs. Vance Carter's spatted shoes.

"No—oh, bring us some lettuce sandwiches and some orange pekoe. I don't think we care for any doughnuts," said Mrs. Carter, impatiently.

Father bolted again, and whispered to Mother, who stood where he had left her, "Lettuce sandwiches and tea, and for Heaven's sake make the tea taste as much like orange pekoe as you can."

The Applebys had no delicately adjusted rule about the thickness of bread in sandwiches. Sometimes Mother was moved to make them very dainty, very thin and trim. But now, because he was in such a fever to please the Carters, Father fairly slashed their last loaf of bread, and slapped in the lettuce, while Mother was drawing tea. In two minutes he was proudly entering with the service-tray. He set it down before the Carters; he fussed with a crumb on the table-cloth, with the rather faded crimson rambler in the ornate pressed-glass vase. Mrs. Carter glanced at him impatiently. He realized that he was being officious, and rushed away.

Mother was sitting by the wide kitchen table, which was scarred with generations of use of cleaver and bread-knife and steak-pounder. The kitchen door was open to the broad land, which flowed up to the sill in a pleasant sea of waving grass. But she was turned from it, staring apprehensively toward the tea-room. Round her swirled the heat from the stove, and restless flies lighted on her cheek and flew off at hectic tangents.

Father tiptoed up to her, smiling. "I've left the door open wide enough so you can see them," he whispered. "Come and take a look at them. Mrs. Vance Carter—gee! And her daughter's a mighty pretty girl—not that I think much of these blouses that are cut so low and all."

"Oh, I wouldn't dare—"

Mother stopped short. Quiet as they were, they could distinctly hear the voices from the other room.

The Carter girl—she who was known as "Pig Carter" at Miss Severance's school—was snapping, "What in the world ever made you come to this frightful hole, mama?"

"Simply because I wanted to stop some place, and I really can't stand that mincing Miss Mitchin and her half-baked yearners and that odious creature with the beard and the ballet skirt, again."

"At least Mitchin's shop is better than this awful place. Why, this might be one of those railroad lunch-rooms you see from a train."

"I'm not so sure this really is worse than the Mitchin creature's zoo, Marky. At least this is a perfect study in what not to do. I fancy it would be a good thing for every interior decorator to come here and learn what to avoid. And, you know, they really might have done something with this place—rather a decent old house, with a good plain fireplace. But then, any one could make a charming room, and only a genius could have imagined this combination—an oak dining-room chair with a wicker table and a cotton table-cloth. I'm sure that Exhibition of Bad Taste—wasn't it? I don't pore over the newspapers as you do—that they held in New York would have been charmed to secure that picture of the kittens and the infant."

All this, conveyed in the Carters' clear, high-bred voices, Father and Mother heard perfectly. . . The picture of kittens and a baby they had bought just after Lulu's birth, and it had always hung above the couch in their living-room in New York.

Margaret Carter was continuing: "I don't mind the bad taste a bit, but I was hungry after motoring all day, almost, and I did want a decent tea. If you could see that horrid Victorian drawing-room at Miss Severance's you could stand even sticky kitties—in a picture. I don't care about the interior decoration as long as Marky's little interior gets decorated decently. But this tea is simply terrible. Orange pekoe! Why, even Miss Severance's horrid Ceylon is better than this, and she does give you cream, instead of this milk of magnesia or soapy water or whatever the beastly stuff is. And to have to drink it out of these horrid thick cups—like toothbrush mugs. I'm sure I'll find a chewed-up old toothbrush when I get to the bottom."

"Don't be vulgar, Marky. You might remember this is Massachusetts, not New York."

"Well, this Massachusetts lettuce—I'm perfectly convinced that they used it for floor-rags before they went and lost it in the sandwiches— and this thick crumby bread—oh, it's unspeakable. I do wish you wouldn't poke around in these horrid places, mama, or else leave me in the car when you are moved to go slumming. I'm sure I don't feel any call to uplift the poor."

"My dear child, I seem to remember your admiring Freddy Dabney because he is so heroically poor. It's very good for you to come to a place like this. Now you know what it's like to be poor, Marky. You can see precisely how romantic it really is."

"Oh, I'll admit Marky is a perfect little devil. But I do want you to observe that she's been brave enough to eat part of her sandwich. Let's go. Where is the nice smiling little man? Let's pay our bill and go."

Twenty feet from the bored Carters was tragedy. Gray-faced, dumb, Father stood by Mother's chair, stroking her dull hair as she laid her head on the crude kitchen table and sobbed. Mechanically, back and forth, back and forth, his hand passed over her dear, comfortable head, while he listened, even as, on the stairs to the guillotine, a gallant gentleman of old France might have caressed his marquise.

"Mother—" he began. It was hard to say anything when there was nothing to say. "It's all right. They're just silly snobs. They—"

Yes, the Applebys could not understand every detail of what the well-bred Carters had said. "Interior decoration"—that didn't mean anything to them. All that they understood was that they were fools and failures, in the beginning of their old age; that they belonged to the quite ludicrously inefficient.

Father realized, presently, that the Carters were waiting for their bill. For a minute more he stroked Mother's hair. If the Carters would only go from this place they had desecrated, and take their damned money with them! But he had been trained by years of dealing with self-satisfied people in a shoe-store at least to make an effort to conceal his feelings. He dragged himself into the tea-room, kept himself waiting with expressionless face till Mrs. Carter murmured:

"The bill, please?"

Tonelessly he said, "Thirty cents."

Mrs. Carter took out, not three, but four dimes—four nice, shiny, new dimes; she sometimes said at her bank that really she couldn't touch soiled money. She dropped them on the table-cloth, and went modestly on her way, an honorable, clever, rather kindly and unhappy woman who had just committed murder.

Father picked up the ten-cent tip. With loathing he threw it in the fireplace. Then went, knelt down, and picked it out again. Mother would need all the money he could get for her in the coming wintry days of failure—failure he himself had brought upon her.

VIII

Having once admitted hopelessness, it was humanly natural that they should again hope that they hoped. For perhaps two weeks after the Carters' visit they pretended that the tea-room was open, and they did have six or seven customers. But late in September Father got his courage up, took out the family pen and bottle of ink, the tablet of ruled stationery and a stamped-envelope, and wrote to Mr. J. Pilkings that he wanted his shoe-store job back.

When he had mailed the letter he told Mother. She sighed and said, "Yes, that is better, after all."

An Indian summer of happiness came over them. They were going back to security. Again Father played the mouth-organ a little, and they talked of the familiar city places they would see. They would enjoy the movies—weeks since they had seen a movie! And they would have, Father chucklingly declared, "a bang-up dinner at Bomberghof Terrace, with music, and yes, by Jiminy! and cocktails!"

For a week he awaited an answer, waited anxiously, though he kept reassuring himself that old Pilkings had promised to keep the job open for him. He received a reply. But it was from Pilkings's son. It informed him that Pilkings, *père*, was rather ill, with grippe, and that until he recovered "no action can be taken regarding your valued proposition in letter of recent date."

Bewildered, incredulous, Father had a flash of understanding that he, who felt himself so young and fit, was already discarded.

Mother sat across the kitchen table from him, pretending to read the *Grimsby Recorder*, but really watching him.

He held his forehead, looked dizzy, and let the letter slip from his fingers. "I—uh—" he groaned. "I—Is there anything I can do for you around the house?"

"Tell me—what did the letter say?"

"Oh, Mother, Mother, maybe I won't get my job back at all! I honestly don't know what we can do."

Running to her, he hid his face in her lap—he, the head of the family, the imperturbable adventurer, changed to a child. And Mother, she who had always looked to him for inspiration, was indeed the mother now. She stroked his cheek, she cried, "Never mind—'course you'll get it back, or a better one!" She made fun of his tousled hair till she had him ruefully smiling. Her voice had a crisp briskness which it had lacked in the days when she had brooded in the flat and waited for her man.

Father could not face another indefinite period of such inactivity as had been sapping him all summer. He longed for the dusty drudgery of Pilkings & Son's; longed to be busy all day, and to bring home news—and money—to Mother at night.

Aside from his personal desires, what were they going to do? They had left, in actual money, less than fifty dollars.

Father did not become querulous, but day by day he became more dependent on Mother's cheer as October opened, as chilly rains began to shut them in the house. When she was not busy, and he was not cutting wood or forlornly pecking away at useless cleanings of the cold and empty tea-room, they talked of what they would do. Father had wild plans of dashing down to New York, of seeing young Pilkings, of getting work in some other shoe-store. But he knew very little about other stores. He was not so much a shoe-clerk as a Pilkings clerk. It had been as important a part of his duties, these many years, to know what to say to Mr. Pilkings as to know what to show to customers. Surely when Pilkings, senior, was well he would remember his offer to keep the job open.

Mother cautiously began to suggest her plan. She spoke fondly of their daughter Lulu, of their grandson Harry, of how estimable and upright a citizen was their son-in-law, Mr. Harris Hartwig of Saserkopee, New York. As Father knew none of these suggestions to have any factual basis whatever his clear little mind was bored by them. Then, after a stormy evening when the fire was warm and they had cheered up enough to play cribbage, Mother suddenly plumped out her plan—to go to Saserkopee and live with daughter till something turned up.

Father shrank. He crouched in his chair, a wizened, frightened, unhappy, oldish man. "No, no, no, no!" he cried. "She is a good girl, but she would badger us to death. She wouldn't let us do one single thing our way. She always acts as though she wanted to make you all over, and I love you the way you are. I'd rather get a job cooking on a fishing schooner than do that."

But he knew Mother's way of sticking to an idea, and he began to persuade himself that Saserkopee was a haven of refuge. Whenever they seemed to be having a peaceful discussion of Lulu Hartwig's canary-

SINCLAIR LEWIS

yellow sweater, they were hearing her voice, wondering if they could tolerate its twangy comments the rest of their lives.

If the weather was clear they sat out in the rose-arbor as though they were soon to lose it. The roses were dead, now, but a bank of purple asters glowed by the laurel-bushes, and in the garden plucky pansies withstood the chill. They tried to keep up a pretense of happiness, but always they were listening—listening.

There were two or three October days when the sea was blue and silver, sharply and brightly outlined against the far skyline where the deep blue heavens modulated to a filmy turquoise. Gulls followed the furrows of the breakers. Father and Mother paced the edge of the cliff or sat sun-refreshed in the beloved arbor. Then a day of iron sea, cruelly steel-bright on one side and sullenly black on the other, with broken rolling clouds, and sand whisking along the dunes in shallow eddies; rain coming and the breakers pounding in with a terrifying roar and the menace of illimitable power. Father gathered piles of pine-knots for the fire, whistling as he hacked at them with a dull hatchet—trimming them, not because it was necessary, but because it gave him something energetic to do. Whenever he came into the kitchen with an armful of them he found Mother standing at the window, anxiously watching the flurries of sand and rain.

"Be a fine night to sit by the fire," he chirruped. "Guess we'll get out the old mouth-organ and have a little band-concert, admission five bucks, eh?" Something of the old command was in his voice. Mother actually needed his comfort against the black hours of storm!

Though they used a very prosaic stove for cooking, the old farm-house fireplace still filled half the back of the kitchen, and this had become the center of their house. Neither of them could abide the echoing emptiness and shabby grandeur of the tea-room. Before the fireplace they sat, after a supper at which Father had made much of enjoying fish chowder, though they had had it four times in eight days. Cheaper. And very nourishing.

The shutters banged, sand crashed against the panes, rain leaked in a steady drip down one corner of the room, and the sea smashed unceasingly. But Father played "My Gal's a High-born Lady" and "Any Little Girl That's a Nice Little Girl Is the Right Little Girl for Me," and other silly, cheerful melodies which even the hand-organs had forgotten.

There was a sense of glaring mounting light through the window which gave on the cliff.

"I wonder what that is," Mother shuddered. "It's like a big fire. I declare it seems as though the whole world was coming to an end to-night." She turned from the window and shivered over the embers, in her golden-oak rocker which Father had filled with cushions.

He kissed her boyishly and trotted over to the window. The fact that they were alone against the elements, with no apartment-house full of people to share the tumultuous night, weakened her, but delighted him. He cried out, with a feeling of dramatic joy.

There was a fire below, on the beach, where there should be nothing but sand and the terror of the storm. The outer edge of the cliff was outlined by the light.

"It's a wreck!" he whooped. "It's the life-savers! Mother, I'm going down. Maybe there's something I can do. I want to do something again! Maybe some poor devil coming ashore in the breeches buoy—help him ashore—Don't suppose I could row—"

He darted at the closet and yanked out his ineffectual city raincoat and rubbers, and the dreary wreck of what had once been his pert new vacation traveling-cap.

"No, no, don't, please don't!" Mother begged. "You couldn't do anything, and I don't dast to go out—and I'm afraid to stay here alone."

But Father was putting on his raincoat. "I'll just run down and see— be right back."

"Don't go a step farther than the top of the cliff," she wailed.

He hesitated. He wanted, more than anything else in the world, to be in the midst of heroic effort. The gods had set the stage for epic action that night, and his spirit was big with desire for bigness. It was very hard to promise to put goloshes upon his winged feet.

But Mother held out her hands. "Oh, I need you, Seth. You'll stay near me, won't you?"

There may have been lordly deeds in the surf that night—men gambling their lives to save strangers and aliens. One deed there certainly was—though the movies, which are our modern minstrelsy, will never portray it. While he strained with longing to go down and show himself a man—not just a scullion in an unsuccessful tea-room—Father stood on the edge of the cliff and watched the life-savers launch the boat, saw them disappear from the radius of the calcium carbide beach-light into the spume of surf. He didn't even wait to see them return. Mother needed him, and he trotted back to tell her all about it.

They went happily to bed, and she slept with her head cuddled on his left shoulder, his left arm protectingly about her.

It was still raining when they awoke, a weary, whining drizzle. And Father was still virile with desire of heroism. He scampered out to see what he could of the wreck.

He returned, suddenly. His voice was low and unhappy as he demanded, "Oh, Mother, it's—Come and see."

He led her to the kitchen door and round the corner of the house. The beloved rose-arbor had been wrecked by the storm. The lattice-work was smashed. The gray bare stems of the crimson ramblers drooped drearily into a sullen puddle. The green settee was smeared with splashed mud.

"They couldn't even leave us that," Father wailed, in the voice of a man broken. "Oh yes, yes, yes, I'll go to Lulu's with you. But we won't stay. Will we! I will fight again. I did have a little gumption left last night, didn't I? Didn't I? But—but we'll go there for a while."

IX

D oggonit, I liked that cap. It was a good one," said Father, in a tone of settled melancholy.

"Well, it wa'n't much of a cap," said Mother, "but I do know how you feel."

They sat in their tremendously varnished and steam-heated room on the second floor of daughter Lulu's house, and found some occupation in being gloomy. For ten days now they had been her guests. Lulu had received them with bright excitement and announced that they needn't ever do any more work, and were ever so welcome—and then she had started to reform them. It may seem a mystery as to why a woman whose soul was composed of vinegar and chicken feathers, as was Lulu Appleby Hartwig's, should have wanted her parents to stay with her. Perhaps she liked them. One does find such anomalies. Anyway, she condescendingly bought them new hats. And her husband, a large, heavy-blooded man, made lumbering jokes at their expense, and expected them to laugh.

"The old boy still likes to play the mouth-organ—nothing like these old codgers for thinking they're still kids," Mr. Hartwig puffed at dinner, then banged his fist and laughed rollingly. He seemed surprised when Father merely flushed and tightened his tie. For all his gross body, Mr. Hartwig was sensitive—so sensitive that he was hurt when people didn't see the humor of his little sallies.

The Hartwigs' modest residence was the last word in cement and small useless side-tables and all modern inconveniences. The furnace heat made you sneeze, and the chairs, which were large and tufted, creaked. In the dining-room was an electrolier made of seven kinds of inimical colored glass, and a plate-rack from which were hung department-store steins. On the parlor table was a kodak album with views of Harry in every stage of absurdity. There was a small car which Mr. Hartwig drove himself. And there was a bright, easy, incredibly dull social life; neighbors who went out to the country club to watch the tennis in summer, and played "five hundred" every Saturday evening in the winter.

Like a vast proportion of the inhabitants of that lonely city, New York, the Applebys were unused to society. It is hard to tell which afflicted them more—sitting all day in their immaculate plastered and varnished room with nothing useful to do or being dragged into the midst of chattering neighbors who treated them respectfully, as though they were old.

Mother begged daughter to be permitted to dust or make beds; Father suggested that he might rake the lawn. But Lulu waggled her stringy forefinger at them and bubbled, "No, no! What would the neighbors think? Don't you suppose that we can afford to have you dear old people take a rest? Why, Harris would be awfully angry if he saw you out puttering around, Father. No, you just sit and have a good rest."

And then, when they had composed to a spurious sort of rest the hands that were aching for activity, the Applebys would be dragged out, taken to teas, shown off, with their well-set-up backs and handsome heads, as Lulu's aristocratic parents.

"My father has been a prominent business man in New York for many years, you know," she would confide to neighbors.

While the prominent business man longed to be sitting on a foolish stool trying shoes on a fussy old lady.

But what could he do? In actual cash Mother and he had less than seven dollars in the world.

By the end of two weeks Father and Mother were slowly going mad with the quiet of their room, and Lulu was getting a little tired of her experiment in having a visible parental background. She began to let Mother do the sock-darning—huge uninteresting piles of Harris Hartwig's faded mustard-colored cotton socks, and she snapped at Father when he was restlessly prowling about the house, "My head aches so, I'm sure it's going to be a sick headache, and I do think you might let me have a nap instead of tramping and tramping till my nerves get so frazzled that I could just shriek."

With this slight damming of her flowing fount of filial love, Lulu combined a desire to have them appear as features at a musicale she was to give, come Saturday evening. Mother was to be in a "dear ducky lace cap" and Father in a frilled shirt and a long-tailed coat which Harris Hartwig had once worn in theatricals, the two of them presiding at the refreshments table.

"Like a prize Persian cat and a pet monkey," Father said.

Against this indignity they frettingly rebelled. Father snarled, "Good Lord! I'm not much older than your precious dumpling of a Harris." It was the snarl of a caged animal. Lulu had them; she merely felt misunderstood when they protested.

Friday morning. The musicale was coming next day, and Lulu had already rehearsed them in their position as refreshment ornaments. Father had boldly refused to wear the nice, good frilled shirt and "movie-actor coat" during the rehearsal.

"Very well," said Lulu, "but you will to-morrow evening."

Father wasn't sure whether Lulu would use an ax or chloroform or tears on him, but he was gloomily certain that she would have him in the shameless garments on Saturday evening.

There was a letter for him on the ten o'clock morning mail. He didn't receive many letters—one a month from Joe Tubbs relating diverting scandal about perfectly respectable neighbors, or an occasional note from Cousin George Henry of Stamford. Lulu was acutely curious regarding it; she almost smelled it, with that quivering sharp-pointed nose of hers that could tell for hours afterward whether Father had been smoking "those nasty, undignified little cigarettes—why don't you smoke the handsome brier pipe that Harris gave you?" She brightly commented that the letter was from Boston. But Father didn't follow her lead. He defensively tucked the letter in his inside coat pocket and trotted up-stairs to read it to Mother.

It was from the Boston agency in whose hands he had left the disposal of the tea-room lease and of their furniture. The agency had, they wrote, managed to break the lease, and they had disposed of the tables and chairs and some of the china. They inclosed a check for twenty-eight dollars.

With the six dollars and eighty-three cents left from their capital the Applebys were the possessors of almost thirty-five dollars!

"Gee! if we only had two or three times that amount we could run away and start again in New York, and not let Lulu make us over into a darned old elderly couple!" Father exulted.

"Yes," sighed Mother. "You know and I know what a fine, sweet, womanly woman Lulu has become, but I do wish she hadn't gone and set her heart on my wearing that lace cap. My lands! makes me feel so old I just don't know myself."

"And me with a granddaddy outfit! Why, I never will dast to go out on the streets again," complained Father. "I never did hear of such a thing before; they making us old, and we begging for a chance to be young, and sitting here and sitting here, and—"

He looked about their room, from the broad window with its resolutely stiff starched net curtains to the very new bureau and the brass bed that looked as though no one had ever dared to sleep in it. He kicked at one of the dollar-ninety-eight-cent rugs and glared at the expanse of smirkingly clean plaster, decorated with an English sporting print composed by an artist who was neither English nor sporting.

"Say," continued Father, "I don't like this room. It's too—clean. I don't dast to wear slippers in it."

"Why, Father, it's a nice room!" marveled Mother. Then, with an outburst of frankness: "Neither do I! It feels like I never could loosen my stays and read the funnies in the last night's paper. Oh, you needn't to look at me so! Many's the time I did that when you were away at the store and I didn't have to sit up and look respectable."

They laughed, both of them, with tender tears. He came to sit on the arm of her rocker and pat her hand.

He said, quietly, very quietly indeed: "Mother, we're getting to be real adventurous. Nothing very old about us, I guess! We're going to sneak right smack out of this house, this very day, and run away to New York, and I'll get a job and we'll stick right there in little old New York for the rest of our lives, so help me Bob!"

"Yes," she said, "yes. I'd like to. But what—uh—what lie could we tell Lulu?"

"Why, Mother, how you talk! Do you know what St. Peter would say to you if he heard you talk about lying? He'd up and jam his halo down over his ears and he'd say, 'You can't come in here, Sarah Jane Appleby. You're a liar. And you know what you can do, don't you? You can go—'"

"Now you see here, Seth Appleby, I just won't have you cursing and swearing and being sacrilegious. I sh'd think you'd be ashamed, man of your age that ought to know better, acting up like a young smarty and cursing and swearing and—"

"And cursing and swearing. Don't forget to put that in, Mother."

He was delighted. It was the first time since September that Mother had scolded him. She was coming back to life again. He tickled her under the chin till she slapped viciously at his finger, then he crowed like a rooster till a shame-faced smile chased away her lively old-dame wrath and, shaking her head with a pretense of disgust, she said, comfortably, "I declare I never did see such a man, not in all my born days." She let him take her hand again, and their expression, half smiles, half musing, was like the sunshine of a calm late afternoon. They were happy. For they knew that, as soon as they should have debated and worried and planned and fussed in a manner appropriate to the great event, they would run away from the overheated respectability of "Lulu's pretty little home."

With enough agony of literary effort to have composed a war article and a column of Household Hints, they sinfully devised a letter for Lulu in which they stated that "a dear old friend, you would not remember him as we have met him since you were married, writes us from Boston that he is sick, and we are going to him, we are stealing out this way because we don't want you to trouble about it, with party coming on to-morrow even'g, know you are so kind you would take all sort of trouble if knew we were going, so just slip away & hope party is great success, Your loving Father & Mother. P.S., May not be back for some time as friend may need us."

In the wreck of their fortunes the Applebys had lost their own furniture, down to the last beloved picture. They had only a suit-case and a steamer-trunk, the highly modern steamer-trunk which Father had once bought for a vacation trip to West Skipsit and the Tubbses. But it required manoeuvering to get even this light baggage to the station.

Mother went nosing about till she discovered that Lulu was going calling that afternoon. Father hired an expressman, who was to be ready to come the instant he telephoned.

Lulu went out at three, and Father stole down-stairs to telephone. But the maid had taken a fancy to dusting the living-room, where the telephone lived. In all her domestic history the maid had never done that before—attest many sarcastic remarks of Lulu.

They had planned to catch the four-o'clock train for New York. Half-past three now. The maid was polishing the silver in the dining-room, which was separated from the living-room only by an open arch. Father dared not telephone, lest she instantly send for Lulu.

Mother tiptoed down and the runaways plotted in whispers. Upon which conspiracy Lulu brightly entered through the front door.

For a second Father had a wild, courageous desire to do the natural thing, to tell Lulu that they were going. But he quailed as Lulu demanded: "Have you tried on the coat and frilled shirt for to-morrow evening yet, papa? You know there may have to be some alterations in them. I'm sure mama won't mind making them, will you, mama! Oh, you two will be so cute and dear, I know everybody will love you, and it will give such a homey, old-fashioned touch that—"

"No, I haven't tried it on yet, and I ain't sure I'm a-going—" Father gallantly attempted.

Lulu glared at him and said, in a voice of honey and aloes, "I'm sure, papa dear, I don't ask very much of you, and when I do ask just this one little thing that I'm sure anybody else would be glad to help me with and me doing my very best to make you happy—"

No! No, no! Father didn't tell her they were going to New York. He was glad enough to escape up-stairs without having the monkey coat tried on him by force.

Their suit case and steamer-trunk stood betrayingly in the middle of the room. With panting anxiety, heaving and puffing, the two domestic anarchists lifted the steamer-trunk, slipped it under the bed and kicked the suit-case into the closet, and sat down to wait for the next train to New York, which left at eleven P.M.

At dinner—such a jolly family dinner, with Mr. Hartwig carving and emitting little jokes, with Harry whining about his homework and Lulu telling the maid what an asphyxiated fool she was to have roasted the lamb too long—Father was highly elaborate in his descriptions of how he had tried on the tail-coat and found it to be a superb fit. As the coat was the personal theatricals-equipment of Mr. Harris Hartwig, who was shaped like the dome of the county court-house, Lulu looked suspicious, but Harry was discovered making bread pills, and she was so engaged in telling him what she thought—Lord, what a thinker the little woman was!—that she forgot to follow the subject.

Out of this life of roast lamb and lies, domesticity and evasions, the Applebys plunged into a tremor of rebellious plotting. They sat in their room, waiting for the Hartwigs to go to bed. Every five minutes Father tiptoed to the door and listened.

At five minutes past ten he shook his fingers with joy. He heard the Hartwig family discursively lumbering up to bed. He stood at the door, unmoving, till the house was quiet, while Mother nervously hung their farewell note on the electric light, and slipped into her overcoat and the small black hat that was no longer new and would scarce be impressive to Matilda Tubbs now.

They had decided to abandon the steamer-trunk, though Mother made a bundle of the more necessary things. The second the house was quiet Father was ready. He didn't even have to put on an overcoat— he hadn't any worth putting on. His old overcoat had finally gone to seed and was the chief thing abandoned with the steamer-trunk. He turned up his coat-collar and slung his muffler about his neck, put his brown slouch-hat impudently on one side of his white head, and stood rejuvenated, an adventurer.

Just below their window was the roof of the low garage, which was built as part of the house. Father opened the window, eased out the suit-case, followed it, and gave his hand to Mother, who creakingly crawled out with her bundle. It was an early November evening, chilly, a mist in the air. After their day in the enervating furnace heat the breeze seemed biting, and the garage roof was perilously slippery. Mother slid and balanced and slid on the roof, irritably observing, "I declare to goodness I never thought that at my time of life I'd have to sneak out of a window on to a nasty slippery shed-roof, like a thief in the night, when I wanted to go a-visiting."

"H'sh!" demanded Father. "They'll hear us and lug us back."

"Back nothing!" snapped Mother. "Now that I've been and gone and actually snook out of a window and made a common gallivanting old hex out of myself this way, I wouldn't come back not if Lulu and Harry and that lump of a Harris Hartwig was all a-hanging on to my pettiskirts and trying to haul me back."

"Oof-flumpf."

This last sound was made by the soft mud beside the garage as Mother landed in it. She had jumped from the roof without once hesitating, and she picked up her bundle and waited quite calmly till Father came flying frog-like through the mist.

They hadn't many minutes to wait for the New York train, but they were anxious minutes. Lest Lulu or the lordly Harris Hartwig descend on them, they nervously lurked in the dark doorway of the baggage-room. With no overcoat, Father shivered—and hid the shiver.

The engine came, glaring in through the mist; the train seemed impatient, enormous, dwarfing the small station. The prodigal parents hastily tugged suit-case and bundle aboard. They found a seat together. They fussily tucked away their luggage. He held her hand firmly, concealing the two hands with a fold of her overcoat. . . You have seen old folk, quite simple and rustic old folk who are apparently unused to travel, sit motionless for hour after hour of train-travel, and you have fancied that they were unconscious of life, of speed, of wonder? So sat Father and Mother, but they were gloriously conscious of each other, and now and then, when he was sure that no one was looking, he whispered: "Old honey, there's nothing holding us apart now no more. We're partners again, and Lord! how we'll fight! I'll go in and I'll take

Pilkings's business clean away from him, I will! Old honey, we're free again! And we're going to see—New York! Lord! I just can't believe it!"

"Yes—why—why, it's our real honeymoon!"

Not till they had ridden for an hour did she demand, "Seth, what *are* we going to do in New York?"

"Why, fiddle! I swear I don't know! But—we'll find something. I guess if we can bamboozle a modern fash'nable daughter we won't be afraid of just New York."

"No!"

Till four in the morning the Applebys sat unmoving, awake and happy. When the train passed the row on row of apartment-houses that mean New York no youngster first seeing the infinitely possible city, and the future glory it must hold for him, was ever more excited than the invading Innocents.

X

With twenty-seven dollars as capital, and a bundle of garments of rather uncertain style as baggage, and the pawn-ticket for a rather good suit-case as insurance, Mr. and Mrs. Seth Appleby established themselves in a "furnished housekeeping room" on Avenue B, and prepared to reconquer New York. It was youth's hopeful sally. They had everything to gain. Yet they were irretrievably past sixty.

You may for many years have been a New-Yorker, yet not know Avenue B, where Jewish apartment-houses and bakeries are sullenly held back by the gas-house district and three-story houses of muddy halls and furtive people who have lost ambition. The genus "furnished housekeeping room" is a filthy box with a stove, a table, a bed, a few seats, many cockroaches, and from one to twenty people, all thrown in and shaken up, like a grab-bag. Here in this world of tired and beaten slinkers the Innocents, with their fresh faces and kindly eyes, excitedly made themselves another home.

With carbolic acid and soap Mother cleaned away much of the smell of former inhabitants, while Father propped up the rusty stove with a couple of bricks, and covered the drably patternless wall-paper with pictures cut from old magazines, which he bought at two for five cents on Fourteenth Street. One of them was a chromo of a child playing with kittens, which reminded him of the picture they had had in more prosperous days. Mother furiously polished the battered knives and forks, and arranged the chipped china on shelves covered with fresh pink scalloped paper. When she was away Father secretly pursued the vulgar but socially conscious sport of killing cockroaches with a slipper.

As the Applebys passed along the hopeless streets, past shops lighted with single gas-jets, or through halls where suspicious women in frowsy wrappers peered at them, they were silent. But in their one room they were hopeful again, and they celebrated its redecoration with music energetically performed by Father on the mouth-organ. Also they ventured to go out to dinner, in a real restaurant of the great city, their city. On Fourteenth Street was a noble inn where the menu was printed in English and Hungarian, where for thirty-five cents each they had soup and goulash and coffee and pudding in three colors, chloroformed beets and vast, pale, uneasy-looking pickles, electric lights in red globes and a tinseled ceiling hung with artificial flowers, the music of a violin and the sight of eager city faces.

SINCLAIR LEWIS

"I'm as excited as a boy with his first pair of red-top boots," declared Father. "Pretty fine to see people again, heh? And pretty soon we'll be dining at the Wal-dorf-As-torya, heh?"

"How you do run on!" said Mother, mechanically, placid dreaminess in her face as she listened to the violin that like a river bore the flotsam of Hungarian and Jewish voices.

Alone, jobless, yet they were so recklessly happy that they went to a ten-cent movie and watched the extreme heroism of a young district attorney with the motionless eager credulity of the simple-hearted.

As soon as they had installed themselves, Father edged shyly into his old haunt, the shoe-store of Pilkings & Son.

He found Son brusquely directing the cleaning out of an old stock of hunting-boots which Pilkings, *père*, had always believed would sell.

Pilkings, *fils*, was bald, and narrow between the eyes. He looked at Father and nodded as though it hurt him.

"I—Is your father around, Mr. Edward?" Father inquired. "I didn't hear from you again—been waiting—thought maybe I'd get a letter—I hope he has recovered—I know how bad the grippe—"

While he was talking he realized that Edward Pilkings was in mourning.

Young Pilkings looked shallowly grieved and muttered, "The old gentleman passed beyond, a week ago Thursday."

"Oh, Mr. Edward, I can't tell you—It's a blow to me, a very great blow. I was with your father for so many, many years."

"Yes—uh—Yes."

"Is there—I wonder if I couldn't send a letter or some flowers or something to your mother?"

"Why, yes, I guess there's nothing to prevent. . . Boy, you be careful of those boxes! What the deuce do you think you're trying to do? There, that's a little better. Try to show some sense about your work, even if you ain't got any." Edward Pilkings's voice crackled like wood in a fireplace.

Desperately Father tried again. "Fact is, Mr. Edward, I've given up my tea-room on Cape Cod. Didn't go so very well. I guess my forty, like the fellow says, is sticking to selling shoes. Mrs. Appleby and I have just got back to town and got settled down and—Fact is, I'd be glad to go back to work."

His hesitant manner invited refusal. It was evident that Mr. Edward Pilkings was not interested.

Shyly Father added, "You know your father promised to keep a place open for me."

"Well, now, I'll tell you, Appleby; it ain't that you aren't a good salesman, but just *now* I'm—well, kind of reorganizing the business. I sort of feel the establishment ought to have a little more pep in it, and so—You see—But you leave your address and as soon as anything turns up I'll be mighty glad to let you know."

For years Father had pityingly heard applicants for jobs disposed of with the request to "leave their addresses."

"No," he said; "no, maybe I'll come in and see you again some day. Good day. Good luck to you, Mr. Edward."

He greeted his old acquaintances among the clerks. They were cordial, but they kept an eye on Mr. Edward Pilkings.

He shivered as he walked out. It was warm and busy in the shoe-store, but outside it was rather chilly for a man with no overcoat—or job. It seemed incredible that he should have found his one place of refuge closed to him.

He walked from shoe-store to shoe-store, hopelessly. "Old-fashioned place," the shoe-men said when he mentioned his experience with Pilkings & Son's. "Be glad to do what we can for you, Mr. Appleby, but just now—"

He had reached the department-store section. Already the holiday rush had begun. Holly was in the windows; Salvation Army solicitors tinkled irritating bells on every corner.

Department stores had always rather bewildered this man of small business, but he inquired for the help-employment bureau in the largest of them, and his shyness disappeared as he found a long line of applicants filling out blanks. Here he did not have to plead with some one man for the chance to work. He was handled quickly and efficiently. On a blank he gave his age, his experience, how much he expected; and a brisk, impersonal clerk told him to return next day.

On that next day the world became wonderful for Father, wonderful and young again, for some one did actually want him. He had a temporary holiday-help job in the leather-goods department, at eight dollars a week.

FATHER'S FIRST DAY OF WORK in the leather-goods department was the most difficult he had ever known. His knowledge of shoes and leather had become purely mechanical; a few glances at new stock and at trade journals had kept him aware of changing styles. Now he had suddenly to become omniscient in regard to hand-bags, portfolios, writing-cases, music-rolls; learn leathers which he had never handled—cobra-seal, walrus, écrasé, monkey-skin. He had to appear placidly official, almost pontifical, when vague ladies appeared, poked clippings from holiday magazines at him, and demanded, "I want something like that." "That" usually depicted articles of whose use he had the most indefinite notions. Other ladies, ponderous ladies, who wanted vast quantities of free advice before purchasing Christmas presents, desired encyclopedic information about sewing-cases, picnic-sets, traveling pillow-cases, telephone-pads, guest-books, and "a cover for my Social Register, and I want you to be sure it's the very latest thing."

He was defenseless. He could not dodge them. Anybody could come up and ask him anything—and did. And while he could learn something about the new leathers, still it was difficult for him to remember the Long Island Railroad time-table well enough to reply instantly when an irate shopper snapped at him, "Do you know what's the next train for Hempstead?"

The most *difficile* woman in a shoe-store has at least a definite, tangible foot to fit. But the holiday crowd were buying presents for persons of whom Father knew nothing—though the shoppers expected him to know everything, from the sizes of their wrists to their tastes in bill-folds. They haggled and pushed and crowded; they wanted it to be less expensive, as well as more blessed, to give than to receive. He spent twenty minutes in showing the entire line of diaries to one woman. She apparently desired to make sure that they were all of them moral or something of the sort. At the end of the time she sighed, "Oh dear, it isn't time for the matinée even yet. Shopping is so hard." And oozed away into the crowd.

Father had started his first day with a superior manner of knowing all about leather and the ways of cranky customers. He ended it with a depressed feeling that he knew nothing about anything, that he couldn't keep up the holiday pace of the younger clerks—and that the assistant buyer of the department had been watching him. He walked home with strained, weary shoulders, but as he turned into the gloomy hallway leading to their room he artificially brightened his expression, that he might bring joy home to Mother, who would have been lonely and anxious and waiting all day.

He pictured her as sitting there, hunched up, depressed. He would bounce in with news of a good day. He tried the door carefully. Mother stood in the middle of the floor, in a dream. In the dimness of the room the coal fire shone through the front draught of the stove, and threw a faint rose on her crossed hands. Taller she seemed, and more commanding. Her head was back, her eyes sparkling. She was clean-cut and strong against the unkempt walls.

"Why, Mother! You look so happy! What is it?"

"I'm going to help! I'm not going to be a lazybones. I've got a job, too! In the toy-department at Regalberg's. And they are going to pay me nine dollars a week. How's that for your stupid old woman?"

"Why—why—you don't need—I don't know as I like—" began the conventional old Father to whom woman's place was in the home whether or not there was a home in which to have a place. Then the new Father, the adventurer, declared, "I think it's mighty fine, Mother. Mighty fine. If it won't be too hard on you."

"I'm going to take you to dinner to-night, instead of you taking me. That is, if you'll lend me a dollar!"

Laughing till they nearly cried, with Father shamelessly squeezing her arm on public thoroughfares, they again plunged into the Roman pleasures of the little tinsel restaurant. And like two lovers, like the telephone-girl in your office and the clerk next door, they made an engagement to meet at noon, next day, in a restaurant half-way between Regalberg's and Father's store.

When she came breathlessly into that beef-stew and paper-napkin restaurant at noon, Mother already had something of the busy, unself-conscious look of the woman who can compete with men. Her cheeks were flushed with walking. Her eyes were young. She glanced about the room, found Father, smiled quickly, and proceeded to order her own lunch in a business-like way.

"They told me to be back in half an hour," she said, "but I don't mind a bit. It's been nice all morning. This is the first time in my life I ever did have all the children to talk to that I wanted. And the sweet toys! Think of me gadding around like this, and enjoying it! I swear to goodness I don't know myself. And what do you think I'm going to do if either of us gets a raise? I'm going to buy you an overcoat!"

Father felt that he didn't know her, either. She did most of the talking at lunch, and hurried cheerfully back to her job, while Father plodded wearily away, speculating as to whether he could keep bustling on tired, stinging feet till six, like the younger holiday help with whom he was in competition.

SINCLAIR LEWIS

He couldn't seem to please the assistant buyer of the department at all, that afternoon, though in his eager way he tried to be the perfect salesman.

On Saturday morning there was a little note for him in which the superintendent was obsequiously Father's servant, and humbly informed Father that his services wouldn't be needed after that day. Would he, if it was quite convenient, call for his pay the following Tuesday, and not fail to turn in his locker-key before leaving the establishment?

The assistant buyer came around and unhappily told Father that they were letting him go because the department was overstocked with younger, liver men. "I'm mighty sorry, and I wish you good luck," he said, with flash of the real man under the smooth, steely exterior.

Father scarcely heard him, though he smiled faintly. He read the note many times as he stumbled home. But he couldn't get himself to show it to Mother till Sunday afternoon, so proud was she of helping him and proving herself a business woman—succeeding in a nine-dollar job while Father, who had once been worth twenty-two good dollars a week, hadn't been able to keep an eight-dollar job. Being quite human, Father felt a scornful envy of her for a minute, when she repeated all the pleasant things that had been said to her. But she was so frank, so touchingly happy, that he could not long harden his heart.

When he told her of his ill-fortune she put her hand to her breast and looked desperately afraid. It was only with a dry gasp that she could say: "Never mind, Seth, you'll find something else. I'm glad you don't have to handle all those silly card-cases and all. And so—so—oh, I do hope you find something."

"You won't think I'm entirely a failure?"

"I won't have you use that word! Don't I know—haven't I seen you for years? Why, I depend on you like—it sounds like a honeymoon, but you're just about my religion, Seth."

But she went to bed very early, to be absolutely certain of being on time at Regalberg's Monday morning.

So BEGAN FOR SETH APPLEBY the haunted days when, drifting through the gray and ghostly city of winter, he scarce knew whether he was a real man or a ghost. Down prison corridors that the city calls streets, among Jewish and Italian firms of which he had never heard, he wandered aimlessly, asking with more and more diffidence for work, any kind of work. His shoes were ground down at the heel, now, and cracked open on one side. In such footgear he dared not enter a shoe-store, his own realm, to ask for work that he really could do. As his December drifted toward Christmas like a rudderless steamer in a fog, the cold permitted him to seek for work only an hour or two a day, for he had no overcoat and his coat was very thin. Seth Appleby didn't think of himself as one of the rank of paupers, but rather as a man who didn't have an overcoat.

He had the grippe, and for a week he never left the house. While Mother proudly carried on the money-earning he tried to do the housework. With unskilled hands he swept—leaving snags of dirt in the corners; he washed—breaking a dish now and then; he even got down on protesting sore knees and sloshed around in an attempt at scrubbing the knotty, splintery floor. He tried to cook dinner and breakfast, but his repertoire consisted of frying—fried eggs, fried bacon, fried bread, fried pork chops, which Mother pretended to like, though they gave her spasms of indigestion. In the richest city in the world he haggled with abusive push-cart peddlers over five cents' worth of cabbage. He was patient, but wrinkled with hopelessness.

With two warm days in succession, and the grippe gone, Father found work as a noontime waiter in a piggery on Third Avenue, where contractors' workmen devoured stew and sour coffee, and the waiters rushed gaspingly about in filthy white aprons. After the lunch hour he washed dishes in soapy water that quickly changed from white to grease-filmed black. For this he received fifty cents a day and his lunch. He hid the depressing fact of such employment from Mother, but religiously saved the daily fifty cents to give to her at Christmas. He even walked for an hour after each lunch, to get the smell of grease out of his clothes, lest she suspect. . . A patient, quiet, anxious, courteous, little aging man, in a lunch-room that was noisy as a subway, nasty as a sewer excavation.

Without admitting it to himself, he had practically given up the search for work. After Christmas—something would happen, he didn't know what. Anyway, they wouldn't go back to their daughter's prison-place unless Mother became ill.

He discovered the life of idle men in New York—not the clubmen, but those others. Shabby, shuffling, his coat-collar turned up and secured with a safety-pin, he poked through Tompkins Square, on sunny days, or talked for hours to hoboes who scorned him as a man without experience of brake-beam and rods, of hoboes' hangouts and the Municipal Lodging House.

SINCLAIR LEWIS

When it was too cold to sit in the park, he tried to make himself respectable of aspect, by turning down his coat-collar and straightening his streaky tie, before he stalked into the Tompkins Square branch of the public library, where for hours he turned over the pages of magazines on whose text he could concentrate less each day that he was an outcast accepting his fate. When he came out, the cold took him like the pain of neuralgia, and through streets that were a smear of snow and dust and blackened remains of small boys' bonfires he shuffled off with timorous rapidity, eying shop windows full of cheap bread, cheap cakes, cheap overcoats, cheap novels on the joy of being poor, all too expensive for him.

Clean and upright and longing to be merry in a dour world, he sank down among the spotted, the shiftless, the worthless. But perhaps when he struck bottom—

He was not quite beaten. He never varied in the wistful welcome he gave to Mother when she dragged herself home from work. But with an increasing humbleness he accepted her as the master of the house, and she unconsciously took the rôle. She petted him and comforted him and worked for him. She announced, with the gaiety that one uses with a dependent small boy, that they would have a wonderful party on Christmas Eve, and with the animation of a dependent child he begged her to tell him about it.

XI

The day before Christmas—an anxious day in Regalberg's department store, where the "extra help" were wondering which of them would be kept on. Most of them were given dismissals with their pay-envelopes. Mother's fate was not decided. She was told to report on the following Monday; the toy-department would be reduced, but possibly they would find a place for her in the children's dresses department, for the January white sale. . . At the very least, they would be glad to give her an excellent recommendation, the buyer told her. More distraught than one stunned by utter hopelessness and ruin, she came home and, as Father had once been wont to do for her, she made her face bright to deceive him.

Under her arm she carried a wonderful surprise, a very large bundle. Father was agitated about it when she plumped gaily into their housekeeping room. At last she let him open it. He found an overcoat, a great, warm, high-collared overcoat.

He had an overcoat—an overcoat! He could put it on, any time, and go about the streets without the pinned coat-collar which is the sign of the hobo. He could walk all day, looking for a job—warm and prosperous. He could find work and support Mother. He had an overcoat! He was a gentleman again!

With tears, he kissed her, lingeringly, then produced his own present, which he had meant to keep till Christmas Day itself. It was seven dollars, which he had earned as waiter at the piggery.

"And we're going out and have dinner on it, too," he insisted.

"Yes, yes; we will. We've been economizing—so much!"

But before they went they carefully cached in the window-box the cabbage he had cooked for dinner.

With a slow luxurious joy in every movement he put on the overcoat. Even in the pocket in which he stuck the seven Christmas dollars he had a distinct pleasure, for his undercoat pockets were too torn, too holey, to carry anything in them. They went prancing to the Hungarian restaurant. They laughed so much that Father forgot to probe her about the overcoat, and did not learn that she had bought it second-hand, for three dollars, and had saved the three dollars by omitting lunch for nearly four weeks.

They had a table at the front of the restaurant, near the violin.

SINCLAIR LEWIS

They glowed over soup and real meat and coffee. There were funny people at the next table—a man who made jokes. Something about the "Yiddisher gavotte," and saying, "We been going to dances a lot, but last night the wife and I wanted to be quiet, so I bought me two front seats for Grant's Tomb!" It was tremendous. Father and Mother couldn't make many jokes, these days, but they listened and laughed. The waiter remembered them; they had always tipped him ten cents; he kept coming back to see if there was anything they wanted, as though they were important people. Father thanked her for the overcoat in what he blithely declared to be Cape Cod dialect, and toasted her in coffee. They were crammed with good cheer when Mother paid the check from a dollar she had left over, and they rose from the table.

Father stood perplexedly gazing at the hat-rack behind them. He gasped, "Why, where—Why, I hung it—"

He took down his old hat with a pathetic, bewildered hesitancy, and he whispered to Mother, "My overcoat is gone—it's been stolen—my new overcoat. Now I can't go out and get a job—"

They cried out, and demanded restitution of the waiter, the head-waiter, the manager. None of these officials could do more than listen and ask heavy questions in bad English and exclaim, "Somebody stole it from right behind you there when you weren't looking."

One of the guests dramatically said that he had seen a man who looked suspicious, and for a moment every one paid attention to him, but that was all the information he had. The other guests gazed with apathetic interest, stirring their coffee and grunting one to another, "He ought to watched it."

The manager pointed at one of the signs, "This restaurant is not responsible for the loss of hats, coats, or packages," and he shouted, "I am very sorry, but we can do nuttin'. Somebody stole it from right behind you there—no one was looking. If you leaf your name and address—"

Father didn't even hear him. He was muttering to himself, "And the seven dollars that I saved for Sarah was in it."

He took Mother's arm; he tried to walk straight as he turned his back on the storm of windy words from the manager.

Once they were away from spectators, on dark Fifteenth Street, Father threw up his hands and in a voice of utter agony he mourned, "I can't do anything more. I'm clean beaten. I've tried, and I've looked for work, but now—Be better if I went and jumped in the river."

She took his arm and led him along, as though he were a child and helpless. She comforted him as well as she could, but there was nothing very convincing to say. As she grew silent her thoughts grew noisy. They shouted separate, hard, brutal sentences, so loudly that she could not hear even the scraping feet of the stooped man beside her. They clamored:

"I can't do anything more, either.

"I don't believe I will be kept on at the store, after all. Only through January, anyway.

"All the money we've got now is the nine dollars they gave me to-day.

"Suppose that's been stolen, too, from our room.

"Suppose I died.

"What would happen to Father if I died? He'd have to go—some dreadful place—poor-house or some place—

"What would happen to me if he died? I'd be so lonely I couldn't stand it. He's always been so dear to me.

"That clerk in the book-department that died from asphyxiation—I wonder if it was accident, after all. They said so, but she was so unhappy and all when she talked to me at lunch.

"'Better jump in the river.' That would be cold and he hasn't got an overcoat. No, of course, that wouldn't make any difference—

"I wonder if gas suicide hurts much?

"If we could only die together and neither of us be left—

"God wouldn't call that suicide—oh, He couldn't, not when there's two people that nobody wants and they don't ask anything but just to be together. That nobody really wants—my daughter don't—except maybe the Tubbses. And they are so poor, too. Nobody needs us and we just want to find a happy way to go off together where we can sleep! Oh, I wouldn't think that would be wrong, would it?"

They were at home. She hastened to burrow among the pile of stewpans for the nine dollars, her week's salary, which she had hidden there. When she found that it was safe, she didn't care so much, after all. What difference would it have made if the money had been gone?

Father staggered like a drunkard to one of the flimsy, straight, uncomfortable chairs. But he got himself up and tried to play on the mouth-organ a careless tune of grassy hills and a summer breeze. While he played he ridiculed himself for such agony over the loss of an overcoat, but his philosophizing didn't mean anything. He had lost the chance of finding work when he had lost the overcoat. He couldn't really think, and the feeble trickle of music had a tragic absurdity. He petulantly threw the mouth-organ on the bed, then himself slumped on the coverlet. His face was grayly hopeless, like ashes or dust or the snow of great cities.

Mother had been brooding. She was only distantly conscious of his final collapse. She said, suddenly, bluntly: "Let's go away together. If we could only die while we are still together and have some nice things to remember—"

Hers was the less conventional mind of the two. He protested—but it was a feeble mumble. The world had come to seem unreal; the question of leaving it rather unimportant.

Much they talked, possibly for hours, but the talk was as confused as the spatter of furniture in that ill-lighted room—lighted by a gas-jet. All that they said was but repetition of her first demand.

While he lay on the bed, flat, his arms out, like a prisoner on a rack, wondering why all his thoughts had become a void in which he could find no words with which to answer her, she slowly stood up, turned out the gas, then again opened the gas-cock.

She hastily stripped off her overcoat and fitted it over the crack at the bottom of the door, where showed a strip of light from the slimy hall without. She caught up the red cotton table-cloth and stuffed it along the window, moving clumsily through the room, in which the darkness was broken only by pallid light that seeped through the window from cold walls without. She staggered over and lay down beside him. Her work was done, and in the darkness her worried frown changed to a smile of divine and mothering kindliness which did not lessen as a thin, stinging, acid vapor of illuminating gas bit at her throat and made her cough.

Father raised his head in stupefied alarm. She drew him down, put his head on her shoulder. She took his hand, to lead him, her little boy, into a land of summer dreams where they would always be together. The Innocents were going their way, asking no one's permission, yet harming no one. . . His hand was twitching a little; he coughed with a sound of hurt bewilderment; but she held his hand firmly, and over this first rough part of the road the mother of tenderness led him pityingly on.

XII

Out of a black curdled ocean where for ages he had struggled and stifled, Seth Appleby raised his head for an instant, and sank again. For longer ages, and more black, more terrible, he fought on the bottom of the ocean of life. He had reached the bottom now. He began to rise. His coughing was shaking him into a half-consciousness, and very dimly he heard her cough, too. He feverishly threw out one hand. It struck the mouth-organ he had thrown upon the bed, struck it sharply, with a pain that pierced to his nerve-centers.

He had the dismaying thought, "I'll never play the mouth-organ to her again. . . We won't ever sit in the rose-arbor while I play the mouth-organ to her. Where is she? Yes! Yes! This is her hand." He was trying to think now. Something said to him, sharply, "Suicide is wicked."

Yes, he reflected, in the tangles of a half-thought, he had always been told that suicide was wicked. Let's see. What was it he was trying to think—suicide wicked—blame the cowards who killed themselves—suicide wicked—No, no! That wasn't the thought he was trying to lay hold of. What was it he was trying to think? Suicide wicked—God, how this cough hurt him. What was it—Suicide? No! He violently pushed away the thought of suicide and its wickedness, and at last shouted, within himself: "Oh, that's what I was thinking! I must play to Mother again! Where is she? She needs me. She's 'way off somewhere; she's helpless; she's calling for me—my poor little girl."

He hurled himself off the bed, to find her, in that cold darkness. He stood wavering under the gas-jet. "Why—oh, yes, we turned on the gas!" he realized.

He thrust his hand up and reached the gas-jet. Then, staggering, feeling inch by inch for leagues along the edge of the cupboard, raising his ponderous hand with infinite effort, he touched a plate, feebly fitted his fingers over its edge, and with a gesture of weak despair hurled it at the window. The glass shattered. He fell to the floor.

Strained with weeks of trying to appear young and brisk in the store, Mother had become insensible before the gas could overcome him, and he awoke there, limp on the floor, before she revived. The room was still foul with gas-fumes, and very cold, for they had not rekindled the fire when they had returned after dinner.

He feebly opened the window, even the door. A passing woman

cried, "Gas in the room! My Gawd! my old man almost croaked himself last year with one of them quarter meters." She bustled in, a corpulent, baggy, unclean, kindly, effectual soul, and helped him fan the gas out of the room. She drove away other inquisitive neighbors, revived Mother Appleby, and left them with thick-voiced words of cheer, muttering that "her old man would kill her if she didn't get a hustle on herself and chase that growler."

With the broken window-pane stuffed up, the gas lighted, and the fire started, the Applebys faced life again, and were very glad. They couldn't have been long under the gas; Father's eons of drowning struggle must have been seconds. Propped up in bed, Mother refused a doctor and smiled—though confusedly, with the bewilderment of one who had felt the numbness of death.

"I'll tell you how it is," cried Father. "We—*Lord!* how glad I am to have you again! It's like this: We felt as if we'd gone the very limit, and nothing ever would come right again. But it's just like when we were a young married couple and scrapped and were so darn certain we'd have to leave each other. That's the way it's been with us lately, and we needed something big like this to get our nerve up, I guess. Now we'll start off again, and think, honey, whatever we do will be a vict'ry—it'll be so much bigger than nothing.

"Let's see. New York doesn't want us. But somewhere there must be a village of folks that does. We'll start out right now, walking through New York, and we'll hunt till we find it, even if we have to go clean out to San Francisco. Gee! think, we're free, no job or nothing, and we could go to San Francisco! Travel, like we've always wanted to! And we won't have any more pride now to bother us, not after—that. I'll play the mouth-organ for pennies! Come on, we'll start for Japan, and see the cherry-blossoms. Come on, old partner, we're going to pioneer, like our daddies that went West."

And he struck up "Susanna" on his mouth-organ.

XIII

The Applebys didn't start for Japan on Christmas Eve. Also, they didn't go defiantly with pack on back through the streets of New York, like immigrants to youth. It took Mother Appleby two days to recover from gas and two more to recover from lifelong respectability, to the end that she should become a merry beggar, gathering pennies while Father piped upon that antic instrument, the mouth-organ.

Father labored with her, and cooked beans for her. She made him agree to get as far from New York as their nine dollars would take them before they should begin to be vagrants. It's always easier to be a bold adventurer in some town other than the one in which you are.

The train took them about eighty miles into New Jersey. They debouched rather shyly, and stood on the station platform in a town consisting of a trust, a saloon, a druggist's, and a general store. The station loafers stared at them. Father would no more have dared play the mouth-organ to these gangling youths than he would have dared kiss a traffic policeman at Forty-second and Fifth Avenue.

They edged around the corner of the station and gingerly stepped off into an ocean of slush, deaf to the yells of the bus-driver who hopefully represented that he would take them practically anywhere in the world for fifty cents.

They were an odd couple. Father had no need of an overcoat, now. He was wearing three shirts, two waistcoats, two pairs of trousers, and three pairs of socks, to say nothing of certain pages of an evening newspaper cunningly distributed through his garments, crackly but warm. He waddled chubbily and somewhat stiffly, but he outfaced the winter wind as he had not done for many weeks. In this outfit he could never have gone the rounds of offices looking for work, but in the open he had the appearance of a hardy woodsman—or at least the father of a woodsman. He wore defiantly the romantic wreck of that plaid cap which he had bought for Cape Cod, which his daughter had sequestered at Saserkopee, and which he had stolen back from her. Also he had a secret joy in the fact that his shirt—that is, his outer and most visible shirt—was a coarse garment of blue flannel, a very virile and knightly tabard with large white buttons, which Mother had never let him wear in public. It was such a noble habiliment as a fireman might have worn, or a longshoreman, or Dan'l Boone.

Mother was almost equally bulky, with an unassayed number of garments, but over them all she wore a still respectable Raglan town coat.

They both carried bundles, and in Father's right hand was a red pasteboard case which protected the mouth-organ. This, as they modestly trotted through the village, he tried to conceal in the palm of his hand, and he glared at a totally innocent passer-by whom he suspected of wanting to hear the mouth-organ.

Mother didn't know of his mental struggles. She was thinking more about her feet. She looked up with mild astonishment when, as they left the town by the highroad southward, Father burst out, "I'll play if I want to, but I can't stand the gawping gumps here."

"Why, Father!" she said, trustingly.

The noontime sun came out. To conceal from his stomach the fact that it was hungry, Father grew boyishly enthusiastic about going Southward. "Gee!" he burbled, "we'll hit down toward Florida—palms and alligators and—and everything—Land of Flowers! What's this hotel?—the Royal Points de Anna? Play the mouth-organ there. Make a hit. Then we'll strike New Orleans and jump to San Francisco. . . Gee! it's a long way between houses along here!"

They approached a farm-yard. Father was tremendously urging himself to play the mouth-organ there, to skip and be nimble, and gain a minstrel's meed. Meaning lunch.

Frowning with intentness, he stopped before the house. Mother meekly halted beside him. She had not lost quite all of the training in self-dependence she had got from a business life, these last weeks, but she looked to him for leadership in the new existence.

Father swung his shapeless pack from his shoulders, set it down on the ground, reluctantly drew his mouth-organ from its case. He became aware that a large, astonished woman was staring from the kitchen window. He stared back. The mouth-organ was left suspended in air. Hastily he stuck it in his pocket and, as though hypnotized, moved toward the kitchen door. He had to give the woman some explanation for encamping in her yard. . . Why! She might have thought that he had intended to make a fool of himself by playing the mouth-organ there!

The woman opened the door curiously, stared over Father's head at Mother, then back at the little man with his pink, cheery face and whiff of delicate silver hair.

"I—uh—I—Could I cut some wood or something for you?" said Father. "Mrs.—uh—Mrs. Smith and I are tramping across the United States—San Francisco and New Orleans and so on—and—"

"Why, you poor things, you must be terribly cold and tired! Think of it! San Francisco! You tell Mrs. Smith to come right in and warm herself by the fire, and I guess I can find some dinner for both of you."

Father scuttled out, informed Mother that she had become Mrs. Smith, and before her slightly dazed mind could grasp it all she was in at a kitchen table near the stove, and eating doughnuts, salt pork, beans, apple pie, and vast cups of coffee. Not but that Father himself was also laying in the food with a lustiness that justified his lumberjack's blue-flannel shirt. From time to time he dutifully mentioned his project of cutting wood, but the woman was more interested in him as a symbol.

In a dim, quite unanalytic way Father perceived that, to this woman, this drab prisoner of kitchen and woodshed, it was wonderful to meet a man and woman who had actually started for—anywhere.

She sighed and with a look of remembering old dreams she declared: "I wish my old man and I could do that. Gawd! I wouldn't care how cold we got. Just get away for a month! Then I'd be willing to come back here and go on cooking up messes. He goes into town almost every day in winter—he's there now—but I stay here and just work."

Father understood that it would have desecrated her vision of the heroic had he played the mouth-organ for pay; perceived that she didn't even want him to chop wood. Mother and he were, to this woman, a proof that freedom and love and distant skies did actually exist, and that people, just folks, not rich, could go and find them.

When she had warmed Mother's feet and given them her wistful good wishes, the woman let them go, and the Smiths recently Applebys, went comfortably and plumply two more miles on their way to Japan.

Father's conscience was troubling him, not because he had taken food from the woman—she had bestowed it with the friendly and unpatronizing graciousness of poor women—but because he had been too cowardly to play the mouth-organ. When Mother had begun to walk wearily and Father had convinced himself that he wouldn't be afraid to play, next chance he had, they approached a crude road-house, merely a roadside saloon, with carriage-sheds, a beer sign, and one lone rusty iron outdoor table to give an air of *al fresco*.

"I'm going over there and play," said Father.

"I won't have you hanging around saloons," snapped Mother.

"Now, Mother, I reckon I wouldn't more than drink a couple of horses' necks or something wild like that."

"Yes, and that's just the way temptation gets you," said Mother, "drinking horses' necks and all them brandy drinks. I wish I'd never tasted that nasty cocktail you made me take last year. I wish I'd joined the White-Ribboners like Mrs. Tubbs wanted me to."

"Well, we'll organize a Hoboes' Chapter of the W. C. T. U. and have meetings under the water-tank at the depot—"

They were interrupted by a hail from the road-house. A large man with a detective's mustache and a brewer's cheeks, a man in shirt-sleeves and a white apron, stood on the porch, calling, "Hey! Mr. and Mrs. Smith! Come right in and get warm."

Father and Mother stared at each other. "He means us," gasped Father.

Mechanically the Innocents straggled across the road.

The saloon-keeper shook hands with both of them, and bellowed: "Lady telephoned along the line—great things for gossip, these rural telephones—said you was coming this way, and we're all watching out for you. You come right into the parlor. No booze served in there, Mrs. Smith. Make yourselves comfortable, and I'll have the Frau cut you up a coupla sandwiches. How'd you leave San Francisco? Pretty warm out there, ain't it?"

He had, by this time, shooed them into the plush and crayon-enlargement parlor behind the barroom. His great voice overawed them—and they were cold. Mother secretively looked for evidences of vice, for a roulette-table or a blackjack, but found nothing more sinful than a box of dominoes, so she perched on a cane chair and folded her hands respectably.

"How's San Francisco?" repeated the saloon-keeper.

"Why—uh—um—uh—how do you mean?" Father observed.

"Yes, I heard how you folks 've tramped from there. How is it, nice climate out there?"

"Why, it's pretty nice—orange groves 'most everywhere. Nice climate," said Father, avoiding Mother's accusing look and desperately hoping she wouldn't feel moved to be veracious and virtuous.

"Hey, Mamie, here's the old couple that 've tramped clear from San Francisco," bawled the saloon-keeper.

A maternal German woman, with a white apron of about the proportions of a cup defender's mainsail, billowed into the room, exclaimed over Mother's wet feet, provided dry stockings and felt slippers for her, and insisted on stuffing both of them with fried eggs and potato salad. The saloon-keeper and a select coterie of farmers asked Father questions about San Francisco, Kansas, rainy seasons, the foot-and-mouth disease, irrigation, Western movie studios, and the extent of Mormonism. Father stuck pretty closely to a Sunday-newspaper description of the Panama-Pacific Exposition for answers to everything, and satisfied all hands to such an extent that they humbly asked him how much danger there was of a Japanese invasion of the Philippines, and how long did he think the great European war would last.

Abashed, prickly with uncomfortableness, Father discovered that the saloon-keeper was taking up a collection for them. It was done very quietly, and the man slipped a dollar and fifteen cents into his hand in so casual a manner, so much as though he were merely making change, that Father took it and uneasily thrust it into his pocket. He understood the kindly spirit of it because he himself was kindly. He realized that to these stay-at-homes the Applebys' wandering was a thing to revere, a heroism, like prize-fighting or religion or going to war. But he didn't psychologize about it. He believed in "the masses" because he belonged to the masses.

As a matter of fact, Father had very little time to devote to meditation when they hit the road again. He was busy defending himself while Mother accused him of having lied scandalously. He protested that he had never said that he had been to San Francisco; they had made that mistake themselves.

"Now don't you go trying to throw dust in my eyes. I just won't have this lying and prevaricating and goings-on. I'm just going to—What's the matter, Seth? You're limping. Are your feet cold?"

And that was the end of Mother's moral injunctions, for Father, with a most unworthy cunning, featured the coldness of his feet till she had exhausted her vocabulary of chiropodal sympathy, after which he kept her interested in the state of his ears, his hands, and the tip of his nose. She patted him consolingly, and they toiled on together, forgetting in the closeness of their comradeship the strangeness of being on an unknown road, homeless, as a chilly sunset spread bands of cold lemon and gray across the enormous sky, and all decent folk thought of supper.

Then everything went wrong with the wandering Innocents.

About supper-time Father made another attempt to get himself to play the mouth-organ, at a mean farm-house which came in sight after a lonely stretch. Mother was sinking with weariness. He hitched the mouth-organ out of its case, but again he shrank, and he feebly said, to a tumble-haired farmer in overalls, "Can I split some wood for you? Mrs. Smith and I are tramping—"

The farmer ungenerously took him at his word. For an hour he kept Father hacking at a pile of wood, while Mother crouched near, trying to keep warm, with his coat over her feet. Father's back turned into one broad ache, and his arms stung, but he stuck to it till the farmer growled: "I guess that'll do. Now don't hang around here."

He handed Father a bundle. Father thought of throwing it at him, but simultaneously he thought of keeping it and consuming its contents. He gasped with the insult. He became angrier and angrier as he realized that the insult applied to Mother also. But before he could think of a smart, crushing, New-Yorkish reply the farmer grumped away into the house.

The Applebys dragged themselves back to the highroad. Father was blaming himself for having brought her to this. . . "But I did try to get a job first," he insisted, and remembered how he had once begged the owner of a filthy shoe-store on Third Avenue for a place as porter, shoeblack, anything.

Their road led them by a clump of woods.

"We'll have a fire here and camp!" cried Father.

He had never made a fire in the open, and he understood it to be a most difficult process. But he was a young lover; his sweetheart was cold; he defied man and nature. Disdaining any possible passer-by, he plunged into the woodland. With bare hands he scooped the light fall of snow from between two rocks, and in the darkness fumbled for twigs and leaves. Gruntingly he dragged larger boughs, piled the wood with infinite care, lighted it tremblingly.

They sat on the rocks by the fire and opened the farmer's bundle. There were cold, gristly roast beef, bread and cheese, and a large, angry-looking sausage.

"Um!" meditated Father; then, "I'll heat up the roast beef." Which he grandly did, on little sticks, and they ate it contemplatively, while their souls and toes relaxed in the warmth, and the black tree-trunks shone cozily in the glow.

"No cockroaches and no smell of fried fish here, like there is on Avenue B," said Father. "And we don't have to go home from our picnic. I wonder why folks let themselves get all old and house-bound, when they could be like us?"

"Yes," said Mother, drowsily.

He hadn't nerved himself to play the mouth-organ, not all day, but now, with the luxury of fire and solitude, he played it, and, what's more, he tried to whistle a natty little ballad which touchingly presented a castaway as "long-long-longing for his Michigan, his wish-again ho-o-ome."

Yet Father wasn't altogether satisfied with his fire. The dry twigs he kept feeding to it flared up and were gone. The Innocents huddled together, closer and closer to the coals. Father gave little pats to her shoulder while she shivered and began to look anxious.

"Cold, old honey?"

"Yes, but it don't matter," she declared.

"Come on, I guess we'd better go look for a place to sleep. I'm afraid—don't know as I could keep this fire up all night, after all."

"Oh, I can't walk any. Oh, I guess it will be all right when I get going again." She tried to smile at him, and with the slowness of pain she reached for her bundle.

He snatched it from her. "I can carry all our stuff, anyway," he said.

Leaning on him, moving step by step, every step an agony of soreness and cold, lifting her feet each time by a separate effort of her numbed will, she plodded beside him, while he tried to aid her with a hand under her elbow.

"There! There's where we'll go!" he whispered, as the shapes of farm-buildings lifted against the sky. "We won't ask permission. We mightn't get it! Like that last farmer. And I won't let you go one step farther. We'll butt right into the barn and sleep in the hay."

"But—do you—think we'd better?"

"We will!"

The mouse-like Father was a very lion, emboldened by his care for her. He would have faced ten farmers terrible with shot-guns. Without one timorous glance he led her to the small side-door of the barn, eased down the latch, lifted her over the sill, closed the door. In the barn was a great blackness, but also a great content. It seemed warm, and was intimate with the scent of cows and hay, alive with the quiet breathing of animals. Father lit a match and located the stairs to the haymow.

Mother was staggering. With his arm about her waist, very tender and reverent, he guided her to the stairs and up them, step by agonized step, to the fragrant peace of the haymow. She sank down and he covered her so deep with hay that only her face was left uncovered.

"Warm, Mother?"

She did not answer. She was already asleep.

Through a night haunted by vague monsters of darkness—and by sneezes whenever spears of hay invaded his indignant city nose—Father turned and thrashed. But he was warm, and he did sleep for hours at a time. At what must have been dawn he heard the farmer at the stalls in the stable below. He felt refreshed, cozily drowsy, and he did a shameless thing, a trick of vagrants and road-wallopers: he put his thumb to his nose, aimed his hand toward the supposititious location of the farmer below, and twirled his outspread fingers in a flickering manner. It is believed that he intended to convey spirited defiance, or possibly insult, by this amazing gesture. He grinned contentedly and went to sleep again. . . Fortunately Mother was asleep and did not see him acting—as she often but vainly defined it—"like a young smart Aleck."

Father awakened from an agitating dream of setting the barn afire, and beheld Mother sitting up amid the hay—an amazing, a quite incredible situation for Mrs. Seth Appleby. She mildly dabbled at her gray hair, which was still neat, and looked across in bewilderment. Like a jack-in-the-box, Father came up out of the hay to greet her.

"How do you like your room in the Wal-dorf-As-torya?" he said. "Sleep well, old honey?"

"Why—why, I must have!" she marveled. "I don't hardly remember coming here, though."

"Ready to tramp on?"

She swore that she was. And indeed her cheeks were ruddy with outdoors, the corners of her eyes relaxed. But she was so stiff that they had hobbled a mile, and Father had shucked several tons of corn in return for breakfast, before she ceased feeling as though her legs were made of extraordinarily brittle glass.

XIV

Sometimes they were fêted adventurers who were credited with having tramped over most of the globe. Sometimes they were hoboes on whom straggly women shut farm-house doors. But never were they wandering minstrels. Father went on believing that he intended to play the mouth-organ and entertain the poor, but actually he depended on his wood-chopping arm, and every cord he chopped gave him a ruddier flush of youth, a warmer flush of ambition.

Most people do not know why they do things—not even you and I invariably know, though of course we are superior to the unresponsive masses. Many people are even unconscious that they are doing things or being things—being gentle or cruel or creative or parasitic. Quite without knowing it, Father was searching for his place in the world. The New York shoe-stores had decided that he was too old to be useful. But age is as fictitious as time or love. Father was awakening from the sleep of drudgery in the one dusty shop, and he was asking what other place there was for him. He was beginning to have another idea, a better idea, which he pondered as he came to shoe-stores in small towns. . . They weren't very well window-dressed; the signs were feeble. . . Maybe some day he'd get back into the shoe business in some town, and he'd show them—only, how could he talk business to a shoeman when he was shabby and winter-tanned and none too extravagant in the care of his reddening hands?

But he was learning something more weighty—the art of handling people, in the two aspects thereof—bluffing, and backing up the bluff with force and originality. He came to the commonplace people along the road as something novel and admirable, a man who had taken his wife and his poverty and gone seeing the world. When he smiled in a superior way and said nothing, people immediately believed that he must have been places, done brave things. He didn't so much bluff them as let them bluff themselves. . . He had never been able to do that in his years as a foggy-day shadow to the late J. Pilkings.

It is earnestly recommended to all uncomfortable or dissatisfied men over sixty that they take their wives and their mouth-organs and go tramping in winter, whether they be bank presidents or shoe-clerks or writers of fiction or just plain honest men. Though doubtless some of them may have difficulty in getting their wives to go.

It was early March, a snowy, blustery March, and the Applebys were plodding through West Virginia. No longer were they the mysterious "Smiths." Father was rather proud, now, of being Appleby, the pedestrian. Mother looked stolidly content as she trudged at his side, ruddy and placid and accustomed to being wept over by every farm-wife.

At an early dusk, with a storm menacing, with the air uneasy and a wind melancholy in the trees, they struck off by a forest road which would, they hoped, prove a short cut to the town of Weatherford. They came to cross-paths, and took the more trodden way, which betrayed them and soon dwindled to a narrow rut which they could scarcely follow in the twilight. Father was frightened. They would have to camp in the woods—and a blizzard was coming.

He saw a light ahead, a shifting, evasive light.

"There's a farm-house or something," he declared, cheerily. "We'll just nach'ly make 'em give us shelter. Going to storm too bad to do much work for 'em, and I bet it's some cranky old shellback farmer, living 'way out here like this. Well, we'll teach the old codger to like music, and this time I *will* play my mouth-organ. Ain't you glad we're young folks that like music and dancing—"

"How you run on!" Mother said, trustingly.

From the bleakness ahead came a cracked but lusty voice singing "Hello, 'Frisco!"

"Man singing! Jolly! That's a good omen," chuckled Father. "All the folks that are peculiar—like we are—love to sing."

"Yes, and talk!" However much she enjoyed Father's chatter, Mother felt that she owed it to her conscience—which she kept as neat and well dusted, now that they were vagrants, as she had in a New York flat—to reprove him occasionally, for his own good.

"Say, this is exciting. That's a bonfire ahead," Father whispered.

They slowed their pace to a stealthy walk. Behind them and beside them was chilly darkness lurking in caverns among black, bare tree-trunks. Before them they could see a nebulous glow and hear the monotonous voice singing the same words over and over.

Mother shrieked. They stopped. A vast, lumbering bulk of a man plunged out from the woods, hesitated, stooped, brandished a club.

"Tut, tut! No need to be excited, mister. We're just two old folks looking for shelter for the night," wavered Father, with spurious coolness.

"Huh?" growled a thick, greasy voice. "Where d'yuh belong?"

"Everywhere. We're tramping to San Francisco."

As he said it Father stood uneasy, looking into the penetrating eye of an electric torch which the man had flashed on him. The torch blotted out the man who held it, and turned everything—the night, the woods, the storm mutters—into just that one hypnotizing ball of fire suspended in the darkness.

"Well, well," gasped the unknown, "a moll, swelp me! Welcome to our roost, 'bo! You hit it right. This is Hoboes' Home. There's nine 'boes of us got a shack up ahead. Welcome, ma'am. What's your line? Con game or just busted?"

"I'm sure I don't know what you mean, young man," snapped Mother.

"Well, if you two are like me, nothing but just honest workmen, you better try and make 'em think you're working some game—tell 'em you're the Queen of the Thimble-riggers or some dern thing like that. Come on, now. Been gathering wood; got enough. You can follow me. The bunch ain't so very criminal—not for hoboes they ain't."

The large mysterious man started down the path toward the glow, and Father and Mother followed him uncomfortably.

"It's a den of vice he's taking us into," groaned Father. "And if we go back they'll pursue us. Maybe we better—"

"I don't believe a con game is a nice thing, whatever it is," said Mother. "It sounds real wicked. I never heard of thimble-rigging. How do you rig a thimble?"

"I don't know, but I think we better go back."

They stopped. The large man turned on them and growled, "Hustle up."

Obediently the Innocents trailed after his dark, shaggy back that, in his tattered overcoat, seemed as formidable as it was big. The glow grew more intense ahead of them. They came into a clearing where, round a fire beside a rude shanty, sat several men, one of whom was still droning "Hello, 'Frisco!"

"Visitors!" shouted the guide.

The group sprang up, startled, threatening—shabby, evil-looking men.

Father stood palsied as grim, unshaven faces lowered at him, as a sinister man with a hooked nose stalked forward, his fist doubled.

But Mother left his side, darted past the hook-nosed man, and snapped: "That's no way to peel potatoes, young man. You're losing all the best part, next to the skin. Here, give me that. I'll show you. Waste and carelessness—"

While Father and the group of circled hoboes stared, Mother firmly took a huge jack-knife away from a slight, red-headed man who was peeling potatoes and chucking them into a pot of stew that was boiling on the fire.

"Well—I'll—be—darned!" said every one, almost in chorus.

"Who are you?" the hook-nosed man demanded of Father. But his voice sounded puzzled and he gazed incredulously at Mother as she cozily peeled potatoes, her delicate cheeks and placid eye revealed in the firelight. She was already as sturdily industrious and matter-of-fact as though she were back in the tea-room.

"I'm Appleby, the pedestrian," said Father. "Wife and I went—Say, ain't she the nicest-looking woman in that firelight! Great woman, let me tell you. We went broke in New York and we're tramping to 'Frisco. Can you take us in for the night? I guess we're all fellow-hoboes."

"Sure will," said the hook-nosed man. "Pleased to have you come, fellow-bum. My name's Crook McKusick. I'm kind of camp boss. The boys call me 'Crook' because I'm so honest. You can see that yourself."

"Oh yes," said Father, quite innocently.

"The lad that the madam dispossessed is Reddy, and this fish-faced duck here is the K. C. Kid. But I guess the most important guy in the gang is Mr. Mulligan, the stew. If your missus wants to elect herself cook to-night, and make the mulligan taste human, she can be the boss."

"Bring me the salt and don't talk so much. You'll have the stew spoiled in about one minute," Mother said, severely, to Crook McKusick, and that mighty leader meekly said, "Yes, ma'am," and trotted to a box on the far side of the fire.

The rest of the band—eight practical romanticists, each of whom was in some ways tougher than the others—looked rather sullenly at Mother's restraining presence, but when the mulligan was served they volunteered awkward compliments. Veal and chicken and sweet potatoes and Irish potatoes and carrots and corn were in the stew, and it was very hot, and there was powerful coffee with condensed milk to accompany it.

Father shook his head and tried to make himself believe that he really was where he was—in a rim of bare woods reddened with firelight, surrounding a little stumpy clearing, on one side of which was a shack covered with tar-paper fastened with laths. The fire hid the storm behind its warm curtain. The ruffians about the fire seemed to be customers in a new "T Room" as Mother fussed over them and kept their plates filled.

Gradually the hoboes thawed out and told the Applebys that they had permission from the owner of the land to occupy this winter refuge, but that they liberally "swiped" their supplies from the whole countryside.

Mother exclaimed: "You poor boys, I don't suppose you know any better. Father, I think we'll stay here for a few days, and I'll mend up the boys' clothes and teach them not to steal. . . You boys—why, here you are great big grown-up men, and you can jus' as well go out every day and work enough to get your supplies. No need to be leading an immoral life jus' because you're tramps. I don't see but what being tramps is real interesting and healthy, if you jus' go about it in a nice moral way. Now you with the red hair, come here and wipe the dishes while I wash them. I swear to goodness I don't believe these horrid tin plates have been washed since you got them."

As Mother's bland determined oration ended, Crook McKusick, the hook-nosed leader, glanced at her with a resigned shrug and growled: "All right, ma'am. Anything for a change, as the fellow said to the ragged shirt. We'll start a Y. M. C. A. I suppose you'll be having us take baths next."

The youngster introduced as the K. C. Kid piped up, truculently: "Say, where do you get this moral stuff? This ain't a Sunday-school picnic; it's a hoboes' camp."

Crook McKusick vaulted up with startling quickness, seized the K. C. Kid by the neck, wrenched his face around, and demanded: "Can that stuff, Kid. If you don't like the new stunt you can beat it. This here lady has got more nerve than ten transcontinental bums put together— woman, lady like her, out battering for eats and pounding the roads! She's the new boss, see? But old Uncle Crook is here with his mits, too, see?"

The Kid winced as Crook's nails gouged his neck, and whimpered: "All right, Crook. Gee! you don't need to get so sore about it."

Unconscious that there had been a crisis, Mother struck in, "Step lively now, boys, and we'll clean the dishes while the water's hot."

With the incredulous gentry of leisure obeying her commands, Mother scoured the dishes, picked up refuse, then penetrated the sleeping-shack and was appalled by the filth on the floor and by the gunny-sacking mattresses thrown in the crude wooden bunks.

"Now we'll tidy this up," she said, "and maybe I can fix up a corner for Mr. Appleby and me—sort of partition it off like."

The usual evening meditations and geographical discussions of the monastery of hoboes had been interrupted by collecting garbage and by a quite useless cleaning of dishes that would only get dirty again. They were recuperating, returning to their spiritual plane of perfect peace, in picturesque attitudes by the fire. They scowled now. Again the K. C. Kid raised his voice: "Aw, let the bunk-house alone! What d'yuh think this is? A female cemetery?"

Crook McKusick glared, but Reddy joined the rebellion with: "I'm through. I ain't no Chink laundryman."

The bunch turned their heads away from Mother, and pretended to ignore her—and to ignore Crook's swaying shoulders and clenching fists. In low but most impolite-sounding voices they began to curse the surprised and unhappy Mother. Father ranged up beside her, protectingly. He was sure there was going to be a fight, and he determined to do for some one, anyway. He was trapped, desperate. Crook McKusick stood with them, too, but his glance wavered from them to the group at the fire and back again, and he was clearing his throat to speak when—

"Hands up!" came a voice from the shadows beyond the fire.

XV

While he was raising his arms so high that his cuffs were pulled half-way down to his elbows, Father was conscious that the hoboes by the fire, even the formidable Crook McKusick, were doing the same. Facing them, in the woods border, was a farmer in a coonskin overcoat, aiming a double-barreled shot-gun, beside him two other farmers with rifles under their arms. It seemed to Father that he was in a wild Western melodrama, and he helplessly muttered, "Gosh! Can you beat it?"

The man with the leveled shot-gun drawled, "I'm the deputy sheriff for this locality and I'll give you dirty bums just five minutes to pick up your duffle and git out, and keep a-going. I guess we don't need you around here. You been robbing every hen-roost for ten miles. Now step lively, and no funny business."

"Stung!" muttered Crook McKusick, hopelessly. "Got us."

Suddenly a downy figure—who might herself have come from a large, peaceful human hen-roost—fluttered straight at the muzzle of the sheriff's shot-gun. It was Mother.

"Hands up, I told juh!" stormed the sheriff, amazedly.

"Oh, look *out*, Mother!" wailed Father, rushing after her, his own hands going down to his sides in his agitation.

"Look out, aunty!" echoed Crook McKusick. "That's a bad actor, that guy."

But Mother continued straight at the gun, snapping: "Don't point that dratted thing at me. You bother me."

The sheriff wavered. The gun dropped. "Who are you?" he demanded.

"Never you mind who I am, young man. I'm responsible for these boys, though. And they promised me they wouldn't do no more stealing. They're going to work for what they get. And they got a right here on this land. They got permission. That's more than you got, I venture, with your nasty guns and all, coming around here—Have you got a warrant?"

"No, I ain't, but you—"

"Then you just step yourself away, young man! Coming here, fairly shaking a body's nerves. I vow, you almost scare me, carrying on—Put down that dratted gun, I told you. You'll either go, Mr. Deputy Monkey, or I'll see your boss, and we'll see what we'll see."

SINCLAIR LEWIS

With which Mother—who was rapidly becoming almost impolite in her indignation over this uninvited visit from a person whom she couldn't find it in her heart to like—seized the muzzle of the gun, pushed it down, and stood glowering at the sheriff, her arms akimbo.

"Well, ma'am, I don't know who you are, but if you got any idee that this bunch of cut-throats is likely to turn into any W. C. T. U. pink-tea party—"

"Now none of your nonsense and impudence and sneering, young man, and be off with you, or I'll see somebody that'll have something to say to you. Illegal goings-on, that's what they are; no warrant or nothing."

One of the sheriff's companions muttered: "Come on, Bill. I think she's the wife of that nosey new preacher over to Cordova."

"All right," said the sheriff. Before he turned away he threatened, "Now if I hear of anything more from you boys, I'll get that warrant, all righty, and you'll land in the calaboose, where you belong."

But the hoboes about the fire cheered derisively, and as the sheriff disappeared in the woods they surrounded Mother in a circle of grins and shining eyes, and the K. C. Kid was the first to declare: "Good for you, aunty. You're elected camp boss, and you can make me perm'nent cookee, if you want to."

"Well, then," said Mother, calmly, "let's get that nasty shack cleaned up right away. I do declare I'm beginning to get sleepy."

Nothing in his life was more to Father's credit than the fact that he did not envy Mother the credit of having become monarch of the camp and protector of the poor. "I'm with you, Mother," he said. "What you want me to do? Let's hustle. Blizzard coming—with a warrant."

Round a camp-fire in the woods a group of men were playing cards, wire-bearded men in rough coats and greasy flannel shirts; but the most violent thing they said was "Doggone it," and sometimes they stopped to listen to the strains of "Dandy Dick and the Candlestick," which a white-haired cheerful old gentleman rendered on the mouth-organ.

Father was perched on a powder-can. His feet were turned inward with comfort and soul-satisfaction, and now and then he jerked his head sideways, with an air of virile satisfaction. The collar of his blue-flannel shirt poked up beside his chin as cockily as the ear of a setter pup. . . Father didn't know it, but he was making believe be King of the Bandits.

Across the fire, in an aged and uncertain rocking-chair, placid as though she were sitting beside a gas-log instead of a camp-fire over-gloomed with winter woods, was Mother, darning a sock and lecturing the homicidal-looking Crook McKusick on cursing and swearing and carryings-on. Crook stared down at her adoringly, and just when she seemed to have penetrated his tough hide with her moral injunctions he chuckled: "By golly! I believe I'll marry and settle down—just as soon as I can find a moll that'll turn into a cute old lady like you, aunty."

"Now, Mr. McKusick," she said, severely, "you want to reform for the sake of reforming, not just to please some girl—not but what a nice sweet woman would be good—"

"Nothing will ever be good for me, aunty. I'm gone. This sweet civilization of ours has got me. The first reform school I went to reformed me, all right—formed me into a crook. I used to show signs of growing up to be fair to middling intelligent, once. But now—nothing to it. You people, though you're twice as old as I am, you're twice as young. You got a chance. Look here, Uncle Appleby, why don't you go out for being one of these famous old pedestrians that get their mugs in the papers? Will you do what I tell you to, if I train you? I've trained quite some pugs before—before I quit."

Mother acerbically declined to learn the art of physical culture. "Me at my time of life learning to do monkey-shines and bending and flapping my arms like a chicken with its head cut off." But Father enthusiastically and immediately started in to become the rival of the gentlemen in jerseys who wear rubber heels in the advertisements and spend their old ages in vigorously walking from the Atlantic coast to the Pacific, merely in order to walk back again.

While his fellow-hoboes about the fire jeered, Father bent over forty times, and raised himself on his toes sixty, and solemnly took breathing-exercises.

Next day he slowly trotted ninety times about the clearing, his chin up and his chest out, while Crook McKusick, excited at being a trainer again, snapped orders at him and talked about form. . . A ludicrous figure, a little old man, his white locks flapping under a mushy cap as he galloped earnestly through the light snow. But his cheeks were one red glow, his eyes were bright, and in his laugh, when he finished, was infinite hope.

If it had been Mother who had first taken charge of the camp and converted it to respectability and digestible food, it was Father who really ran it, for he was the only person who could understand her and Crook McKusick and the sloppy Kid all at once.

Crook McKusick had long cultivated a careful habit of getting drunk once a week. But two weeks after the coming of the Applebys he began to omit his sprees, because Mother needed him to help her engineer variations of the perpetual mulligan, and Father needed him for his regular training.

To the training Crook added a course in psychology. As a hobo he was learned in that science. The little clerk, the comfortable banker, the writer of love-stories—such dull plodders have their habits all set out for them. But the hobo, who has to ride the rods amid flying gravel to-day, and has to coax food out of a nice old lady to-morrow, must have an expert working knowledge of psychology if he is to climb in his arduous profession.

Father and Mother had started out from New York on a desperate flight, with no aspirations beyond the hope that they might be able to make a living. It was the hobo, Crook McKusick, who taught Father that there was no reason why, with his outdoor life and his broadened experience, he should not be a leader among men wherever he went; be an Edward Pilkings and a Miss Mitchin, yea, even a Mrs. Lulu Hartwig, instead of a meek, obedient, little Seth Appleby. It was Crook who, out of his own experience in doing the unusual, taught Father that it was just as easy to be unusual, to live a life excitedly free, as to be a shop-bound clerk. Adventure, like fear of adventure, consisted in going one step at a time, keeping at it, forming the habit. . . So, an outcast among outcasts, grubbily bunked in a camp of hoboes, talking to a filthy lean man with an evil hooked nose, Seth Appleby began to think for himself, to the end that he should be one of the class that rules and is unafraid.

The amiable boarders at Hoboes' Home didn't at all mind Mother's darning their socks. They didn't much mind having her order them to wash their faces at a hole through the ice in the near-by creek before coming to dinner. But it took her many days to get them used to going off to work for money and supplies. Yet every day half the camp grumblingly disappeared to shuck corn, mend fences, repair machinery, and they came back with flour, potatoes, meat, coffee, torn magazines, and shirts. Father regularly went out to work with them, and was the first to bring water, to cut wood. They all took a pride in the camp. They kept the bunk-house scrubbed, and inordinately admired the new mattresses, stuffed with fresh straw and covered with new calico, which

Mother made for them. In the evenings the group about the camp-fire was not so very different from any other happy family—except that there was an unusually large proportion of bright eyes and tanned faces.

But when spring cleared the snow away, made the bare patches of earth quiver with coming life, sent the crows and an occasional flock of ducks overhead—vagrants of the air, calling to their vagrant brothers about the fire—there was no sorrow in the break-up of the family, but only a universal joy in starting off for new adventures.

THAT HONEST WORKMAN, "STRUCK DUMB," disappeared one afternoon, telling Crook that he heard of much building at Duluth.

Crook laughed when Mother admired Mr. Struck Dumb's yearning for creative toil. "That guy," Crook declared, "is an honest workman except that he ain't honest and he won't work. He'll last about two days in Duluth, and then he'll pike for Alberta or San Diego or some place. He's got restless feet, same like me."

The K. C. Kid and Reddy jigged and shouted songs all one evening, and were off for the north. At last no one but Father and Mother and Crook was left. And they, too, were star-eyed with expectation of new roads, new hills. They sat solemnly by the fire on their last evening. Mother was magnificent in a new cloak, to buy which Father had secretly been saving pennies out of the dimes that he had earned by working about the country.

Usually Crook McKusick was gravely cynical when he listened to Father's cataract of excited plans, but he seemed wistful to-night, and he nodded his head as though, for once, he really did believe that Father and Mother would find some friendly village that would take them in.

Father was telling a story so ardently that he almost made himself believe it: Some day, Mother and he would be crawling along the road and discover a great estate. The owner, a whimsical man, a lonely and eccentric bachelor of the type that always brightens English novels, would invite them in, make Father his steward and Mother his lady housekeeper. There would be a mystery in the house—a walled-off room, a sound of voices at night in dark corridors where no voices could possibly be, a hidden tragedy, and at last Father and Mother would lift the burden from the place, and end their days in the rose-covered dower-house. . . Not that Father was sure just what a dower-house was, but he was quite definite and positive about the rose-covering.

SINCLAIR LEWIS

"How you run on," Mother yawned.

"Aw, let him," Crook cried, with sudden fierceness. "My Gawd! you two almost make me believe that there is such a thing as faith left in this dirty old world, that's always seemed to me just the back of an eternal saloon. Maybe—maybe I'll find my ambition again. . . Well—g' night."

When with their pack and their outlooking smiles the Applebys prepared to start, next day, and turned to say good-by to Crook, he started, cried, "I will!" and added, "I'm coming with you, for a while!"

For two days Crook McKusick tramped with them, suiting his lean activity, his sardonic impatience, to their leisurely slowness. He called to the blackbirds, he found pasque-flowers for them, and in the sun-baked hollows between hillocks coaxed them to lie and dream.

But one morning they found a note:

DEAR AUNTY AND UNCLE

Heard a freight-train whistle and I'm off. But some day I'll find you again. I'll cut out the booze, anyway, and maybe I'll be a human being again. God bless you babes in the woods.

C. McK.

"The poor boy! God will bless him, too, and keep him, because he's opened his heart again," whispered Mother. "Are we babes in the woods, Seth? I'd rather be that than a queen, long as I can be with you."

East and west, north and south, the hoboes journeyed, and everywhere they carried with them fables of Mr. and Mrs. Seth Appleby, the famous wanderers, who at seventy, eighty, ninety, were exploring the world. Benighted tramps in city lock-ups, talking to bored police reporters, told the story, and it began to appear in little filler paragraphs here and there in newspapers.

Finally a feature-writer on a Boston paper, a man with imagination and a sense of the dramatic, made a one-column Sunday story out of the adventures of Mr. and Mrs. Appleby. He represented them as wealthy New-Yorkers who were at once explorers and exponents of the simple life. He said nothing about a shoe-store, a tea-room, a hobo-camp.

The idea of these old people making themselves a new life caught many imaginations. The Sunday story was reprinted and reprinted till the source of it was entirely forgotten. The names of the Applebys became stock references in many newspaper offices—Father even had a new joke appended to his name, as though he were an actor or an author or Chauncey Depew.

The Applebys were largely unconscious of their floating fame. But as they tramped westward through West Virginia, as the flood tide of spring and the vigor of summer bore them across Ohio and into Indiana, they found that in nearly every town people knew their names and were glad to welcome them as guests instead of making them work for food. When Father did insist on cutting wood or spading a garden, it was viewed as a charming eccentricity in him, a consistent following of the simple life, and they were delighted when he was so whimsical as to accept pay for his work.

But he never played the mouth-organ—except to Mother!

XVI

They were in Indiana, now. They had saved up six dollars and twenty cents, despite the fact that Father had overborne her caution and made her dine at a lunch-room, now and then, or sleep at a hotel, while he cheerfully scavenged in the neighborhood.

The shoes he had bought in West Virginia were impossible. They had been mended and resoled, but the new soles had large concentric holes. Mother discovered the fact, and decisively took the problem out of his hands. He was going to take that six dollars and twenty cents, he was, and get new shoes. It was incredible luxury.

He left Mother at a farm-house. He stood meditatively before the window of a shoe-store in Lipsittsville, Indiana. Lawyer Vanduzen, who read the papers, guessed who he was, and imparted the guess to the loafers in front of the Regal Drug Store, who watched him respectfully.

Inside the shoe-store, the proprietor was excited. "Why," he exclaimed to his assistant, "that must be Appleby, the pedestrian—fellow you read so much about—the Indianapolis paper said just this morning that he was some place in this part of the country—you know, the fellow who's tramped all over Europe and Asia with his wife, and is bound for San Francisco now." His one lone clerk, a youth with adenoids, gaped and grunted. It was incredible to him that any one should walk without having to.

Father was aware of the general interest, and as he was becoming used to his rôle as public character, he marched into the store like the Lord Mayor of London when he goes shopping in his gold coach with three men and a boy in powdered wigs carrying his train.

The proprietor bowed and ventured: "Glad to see you with us, Mr. Appleby. It is Mr. Appleby, isn't it?"

"Uh-huh," growled Father.

"Well, well! Tramping like yours is pretty hard on the footgear, and that's a fact! Well, well! Believe me, you've come to just the right store for sport shoes. We got a large line of smart new horsehide shoes. Dear me! Tut, tut, tut, tut! What a pity, the way the tramping has worn out yours—fine shoe, too, I can see that. Well, well, well, well! how it surely does wear out the shoes, this long tramping. Peter, bring a pair of those horsehide shoes for Mr. Appleby. Nice, small, aristocratic foot, Mr. Appleby. If you worked in a shoe-store you'd know how uncommon—"

"Huh! Don't want horsehide. Try a pair o' those pigskin shoes over there that you got a sale on."

"Well, well, you do know what you want," fawned the shoeman. "Those pigskins are a very fine grade of shoe, and very inexpensive, very good for tramping—"

"Yump. They'll do."

"Going to be with us long?" inquired the shoeman, after trying on the shoes and cursing out Peter, the adenoidic clerk, in an abstracted, hopeless manner.

"Nope." Father was wonderfully bored and superior. Surely not this Seth Appleby but a twin of his, a weak-kneed inferior twin, had loafed in Tompkins Square and wavered through the New York slums, longing for something to do. He didn't really mean to be curt, but his chief business in life was to get his shoes and hurry back to Mother, who was waiting for him, a mile from town, at a farm where the lordly Father had strung fence-wire and told high-colored stories for his breakfast.

The fascinated shoeman hated to let him go. The shoeman knew few celebrities, and a five-mile motor ride was his wildest adventure. But by the light of a secret lamp in the bathroom, when his wife supposed him to have gone to bed, he breathlessly read the *Back o' the Beyond Magazine*, and slew pirates with a rubber sponge, and made a Turkish towel into a turban covered with quite valuable rubies, and coldly defied all the sharks in the bathtub. He was an adventurer and he felt that Father Appleby would understand his little-appreciated gallantry. He continued, "The madam with you?"

"Yump."

"Say—uh—if I may be so bold and just suggest it, we'd be honored if you and the madam could take dinner at our house and tell us about your trip. The wife and me was talking about it just this morning. The wife said, guessed we'd have to pike out and do the same thing! Hee, hee! And Doc Schergan—fine bright man the doc, very able and cultured and educated—he's crazy to meet you. We were talking about you just this morning—read about your heading this way, in the Indianapolis paper. Say," he leaned forward and whispered, after a look at his clerk which ought to have exterminated that unadventurous youth—"say, is it true what they say, that you're doing this on a ten-thousand-dollar bet?"

"Well," and Father thawed a little, "that's what they're all saying, but, confidentially, and don't let this go any further, it isn't as much as that. This is between you and I, now."

"Oh yessss," breathed the flattered shoeman. "There's your shoes, Mr. Appleby. Four dollars, please. Thank you. And let me tell you, confidentially, you got the best bargain in the store. I can see with half an eye you've learned a lot about shoes. I suppose it's only natural, tramping and wearing them out so fast and visiting the big burgs and all—"

"Huh! Ought to know shoes. Used to be in business. Pilkings & Son's, little old New York. Me and old Pilky practically started the business together, as you might say."

"Well, well, well, well!" The shoeman stared in reverent amazement. Then, as he could think of nothing further to say, he justly observed, "Well!"

"Yump. That reminds me. Make that boy of yours rearrange that counter case there. Those pink-satin evening slippers simply lose all their display value when you stick those red-kid bed-slippers right up ferninst them that way.

"Yes, yes, that's so. I'm much obliged to you for the tip, Mr. Appleby. That's what it is to be trained in a big burg. But I'll have to rearrange it myself. That boy Peter is no good. I'm letting him go, come Saturday."

"That so?" said Father; then, authoritatively: "Peter, my boy, you ought to try to make good here. Nothing I'd like better—if I had the time—than to grow up in a shoe-store in a nice, pretty village like this."

"Yes, that's what I've told him many's the time. Do you hear what Mr. Appleby says, Peter? . . . Say, Mr. Appleby, does this town really strike you as having the future for the shoe business?"

"Why, sure."

"Are you ever likely to think about going back into the shoe business again, some day? 'Course," apologetically, "you wouldn't ever want to touch anything in as small a burg as this, but in a way it's kind of a pity. I was just thinking of how the youngsters here would flock to have you give 'em your expert advice as a sporting gentleman, instead of hanging around that cheap-John shoe-store that those confounded worthless Simpson boys try to run."

Father carefully put down the bundle of his new shoes, drew a long breath, then tried to look bored again. Cautiously: "Yes, I've thought some of going back into business. 'Course I'd hate to give up my exploring and all, but—Progress, you know; hate to lay down the burden of big affairs after being right in the midst of them for so long." Which was a recollection of some editorial Father had read in a stray roadside newspaper. "And you mustn't suppose I'd be sniffy about Lipsittsville. No, no; no, indeed. Not at all. I must say I don't know when I've seen a more wide-awake, pretty town—and you can imagine how many towns I must have seen. Maples and cement walks and nice houses and—uh—wide-awake town. . . Well, who knows! Perhaps some day I might come back here and talk business with you. Ha, ha! Though I wouldn't put in one cent of capital. No, sir! Not one red cent. All my money is invested with my son-in-law—you know, Harris Hartwig, the famous chemical works. Happen to know um?"

"Oh yes, indeed! Harry Sartwig. I don't know him *personally*, but of course I've heard of him. Well, I do wish you'd think it over, some day, Mr. Appleby. Indeed I understand about the capital. If you and me ever did happen to come to terms, I'd try to see my way clear to giving you an interest in the business, in return for your city experience and your expert knowledge and fame and so on as an explorer—not that we outfit so many explorers here. Hee, hee!"

"Well, maybe I'll think it over, some day. Well—well, maybe I'll see you again before I get out of town. I'm kind of planning to stick around here for a day or two. I'll talk over the suggestion with Mrs. Appleby. Me, I could probably call off my wager; but she is really the one that you'd have to convince. She's crazy for us to hike out and tramp clear down into Mexico and Central America. Doesn't mind bandits and revolutions no more than you and I would a mouse."

In his attempt to let people bluff themselves and accept him as a person to be taken seriously, Father kept on trying to adhere to the truth. But certainly this last statement of his was the grossest misrepresentation of Mother's desires. Mother Appleby, with her still unvanquished preference for tea and baths, did not have the slightest desire to encounter bandits, snakes, deserts, or cacti of any variety.

"Well, look *here*, Mr. Appleby; if you are going to be around, couldn't you and the madam come to dinner, as I was so bold as to suggest awhile ago? That would give us a chance to discuss things. Aside from any future business dicker between you and me personally, I'd like to show you just why Lipsittsville is going to be a bigger town than Freiburg or Taormina or Hongkong or Bryan or any of the other towns in the county, let 'em say what they like! Or couldn't you come to supper to-night? Then we could let the ladies gossip, and I'll have Doc Schergan come in, and maybe him and me between us could persuade you to think of taking a partnership with me—wouldn't cost you a cent of capital, neither. Why, the doc was saying, just this morning, when we was speaking of having read about you in the paper—he was saying that you were the kind of man we need for president of our country club, instead of some dude like that sissified Buck Simpson. Buck is as punk an athlete as he is a shoeman, and, believe me, Mr. Appleby, we've got the makings of a fine country club. We expect to have a club-house and tennis-courts and golluf-links and all them things before long. We got a croquet-ground right now! And every Fourthajuly we all go for a picnic. Now can't the madam come? Make it supper this evening. But, say, I want to warn you that if we ever did talk business, I don't see how I could very well offer you more than a forty-per-cent. interest, in any case."

"No," growled Father, "wouldn't take over a third interest. Don't believe in demanding too much. Live and let live, that's my motto."

"Yes, sir, and a fine motto it is, too," admired the shoeman.

"What time is supper?"

". . . AND BEFORE I GET THROUGH with it I'll own a chain of shoe-stores from here to Indianapolis," said Father. "I'll be good for twenty years' more business, and I'll wake this town up."

"I do believe you will, Father. But I just can't believe yet that you've actually signed the contract and are a partner," Mother yearned. "Why, it ain't possible."

"Guess it is possible, though, judging by this hundred dollar advance," Father chuckled. "Nice fellow, that shoeman—or he will be when he gets over thinking I'm a tin god and sits down and plays crib like I was an ordinary human being. . . We ought to have larger show-windows. We'll keep Peter on—don't want to make the boy lose his job on account of me. Give him another chance. . . I'm just wambling, Mother, but I'm so excited at having a job again—"

With tiny pats of her arm, he stalked the street, conscious of the admiring gaze of the villagers, among whom ran the news that the famous explorer was going to remain with them.

When the landlord himself had preceded them up-stairs to the two rooms which the shoeman had engaged for the Applebys at the Star Hotel, Father chuckled: "Does it look more possible, now, with these rooms, eh? Let's see, we must get a nice little picture of a kitten in a basket, to hang over that radiator. Drat the landlord, I thought he'd stick here all evening, and—I want to kiss you, my old honey, my comrade!"

XVII

The Lipsittsville Pioneer Shoe Store found Mr. Seth Appleby the best investment it had ever made. The proprietor was timorous about having given away thirty-three per cent. of his profits. But Mr. Appleby did attract customers—from the banker's college-bred daughter to farmers from the other side of the Lake—and he really did sell more shoes. He became a person of lasting importance.

In a village, every clerk, every tradesman, has something of the same distinctive importance as the doctors, the lawyers, the ministers. It really makes a difference to you when Jim Smith changes from Brown's grocery to Robinson's, because Jim knows what kind of sugar-corn you like, and your second cousin married Jim's best friend. Bill Blank, the tailor, is not just a mysterious agent who produces your clothes, but a real personality, whose wife's bonnet is worth your study, even though you are the wife of the mayor. So to every person in Lipsittsville Mr. Seth Appleby was not just a lowly person on a stool who helped one in the choice of shoes. He was a person, he was their brother, to be loved or hated. If he had gone out of the shoe business there would have been something else for him to do—he would have sold farm machinery or driven on a rural mail route or collected rents, and have kept the same acquaintances.

It was very pleasant to Father to pass down the village street in the sun, to call the town policeman "Ben" and the town banker "Major" and the town newspaperman "Lym," and to be hailed as "Seth" in return. It was diverting to join the little group of G. A. R. men in the back of the Filson Land and Farms Company office, and have even the heroes of Gettysburg pet him as a promising young adventurer and ask for his tales of tramping.

Father was rather conscience-stricken when he saw how the town accepted his pretense of being an explorer, but when he tried to tell the truth everybody thought that he was merely being modest, and he finally settled down contentedly to being a hero, to the great satisfaction of all the town, which pointed out to unfortunate citizens of Freiburg and Hongkong and Bryan and other rival villages that none of them had a real up-to-date hero with all modern geographical improvements. In time, as his partner, the shoeman, had predicted, Father was elected president of the clubless country club, and organized a cross-country hike in which he outdistanced all the others, including the young and boastful Buck Simpson.

He was slowly recognized as being "in society." To tell the truth, most of Lipsittsville was in society, but a few citizens weren't—Barney Bachschluss, the saloon-keeper; Tony, who sawed wood and mowed lawns; the workmen on the brick-yard and on the railway. Father was serenely established upon a social plane infinitely loftier than theirs.

He wore a giddy, spotted, bat-wing tie, and his grand good gray trousers were rigidly creased. He read editorials in the Indianapolis paper and discussed them with Doc Schergan at the drug-store.

The only trouble was that Mother had nothing to do. She was discontented, in their two rooms at the Star Hotel. No longer could she, as in her long years of flat life in New York, be content to sit dreaming and reading the paper. She was as brisk and strong and effective as Father. Open woods and the windy road had given her a restless joy in energy. She made a gown of gray silk and joined the Chautauqua Circle, but that was not enough.

On an evening of late August, when a breeze was in the maples, when the sunset was turquoise and citron green and the streets were serenely happy, Father took her out for a walk. They passed the banker's mansion, with its big curving screened porch, and its tower, and brought up at a row of modern bungalows which had just been completed.

"I wanted you to see these," said Father, "because some time—this is a secret I been keeping—some time I guess we'll be able to rent one of these! Don't see why we can't early next year, the way things are going!"

"Oh, Father!" she said, almost tearfully.

"Would you like it?"

"Like it! With a real house and something to keep my hands busy! And maybe a kitty! And I would make you tea (I'm so tired of hotel food!) and we would sit out here on the porch—"

"Yes, you'd have old Mr. Seth Appleby for tea-room customer. He's better 'n anybody they got on Cape Cod!"

"Yes, and you *are* better, too, Father!"

"You old honeymooner! Say, I've got an idea. I wonder if we couldn't sneak in a look inside of one of these bungalows. Let's try this door."

He shook the door-knob of a bungalow so new that laths and mortar were still scattered about the yard. The door was locked. He tried the windows as well. But he could not get in. Three other bungalows they tried, and the fourth, the last of the row, was already occupied. But they did steal up on the porch of one bungalow, and they exclaimed like children when they beheld the big living-room, the huge fireplace, the built-in shelves and, beyond the living-room, what seemed to be the dining-room, with an enormous chandelier which may not, perhaps, have been of the delicate reticence of a silver candlestick, but whose jags and blobs of ruby and emerald and purple glass filled their hearts with awe.

"We *will* get one of these houses!" Father vowed. "I thought you'd like them. I swear, I'll cut out my smoking, if necessary. Say! Got another idea! I wonder if we couldn't make up some excuse and butt into the bungalow that's been rented, and see how it looks furnished. I understand there's some new-comers living there. We'll sort of make them a neighborly call."

"Oh, do you think we ought to?"

Mother, she who had faced a sheriff's shot-gun, was timorous about facing an irate matron, and she tagged hesitatingly after Father as he marched along the row of bungalows, up the steps of the one that was rented, and rang the bell.

The door was opened by a maid, in a Lipsittsville version of a uniform.

"Lady or gent o' the house in?" asked Father, airily sticking his new derby on one side of his head and thrusting a thumb in an armhole, very impudent and fresh and youthful.

"No, sir," said the maid, stupidly.

Mother sighed. To tell the truth, she had wanted to see the promised land of this bungalow.

"Well, say, girl, Mrs. Appleby and I are thinking of renting one of these here bungalonies, like the fellow says, and I wonder if we could take a look at this house, to see how it looks furnished?"

The maid stared dumbly at him, looked suspiciously at Mother. Apparently she decided that, though the flamboyant Father was likely to steal everything in the house, Mother was a person to be trusted, and she mumbled, "Yass, I gass so."

Father led the way in, and Mother stumbled over every possible obstacle, so absorbed was she by the intimate pleasantness which furniture gave to this big living-room—as large as the whole of their flat in New York. Actually, the furniture wasn't impressive—just a few good willow chairs, a big couch, a solid table. There were only two or three pictures, one rug, and, in the built-in shelves, no books at all. But it had space and cheerfulness; it was a home.

SINCLAIR LEWIS

"Here's the dining-room, with butler's pantry, and that door on the right looks like it might be a bedroom," Father announced, after a hasty exploration, while the maid stared doubtfully. He went on, half whispering, "Let's peep into the bedroom."

"No, no, we mustn't do that," Mother insisted, but regretfully. For she was already wondering where, if she were running things, she would put a sewing-machine. She had always agreed with Matilda Tubbs that sewing-machines belonged in bedrooms.

While the maid shadowed him and Mother opened her mouth to rebuke him, Father boldly pushed open the door on the right. He had guessed correctly. It was a bedroom. Mother haughtily stayed in the center of the living-room, but she couldn't help glancing through the open door, and she sighed enviously as she saw the splendor of twin beds, with a little table and an electric light between them, and the open door of a tiled bathroom. It was too much that the mistress of the house should have left her canary-yellow silk sweater on the foot of one bed. Mother had wanted a silk sweater ever since she had beheld one flaunted on Cape Cod.

Father darted out, seized her wrists, dragged her into the bedroom, and while she was exploding in the lecture he so richly deserved she stopped, transfixed. Father was pointing to a picture over one bed, and smiling strangely.

The picture was an oldish one, in a blackened old frame. It showed a baby playing with kittens.

"Why!" gasped Mother—"why—why, it's just like the picture—it *is* the picture—that we got when Lulu was born—that we had to leave on the Cape."

"Yump," said Father. He still smiled strangely. He pointed at the table between the twin beds. On the table was a little brown, dusty book. Mother gazed at it dazedly. Her step was feeble as she tottered between the beds, picked up the book, opened it. It was the New Testament which she had had since girlhood, which she had carried all through their hike, which she supposed to be in their rooms back at the Star Hotel.

There was a giggle from the doorway, and the apparently stupid maid was there, bowing.

"Lena, has our trunk come from the hotel?" Father asked.

"Yessir, I just been sneaking it in the back way. Welcome home, mum," said the maid, and shut the door—from the other side.

Mother suddenly crumpled, burrowed her head against Father's shoulder and sobbed: "This is ours? Our own? Now?"

"Yes, Mother, it sure am ours." Father still tried to speak airily, but in his voice were passion and a grave happiness. "It's ours—*yours*! And every stick of the furniture more than half paid for already! I didn't tell you how well we're doing at the store. Say, golly, I sure did have a time training Lena to play the game, like she didn't know us. She thought I was plumb nutty, at first!"

"And I have a maid, too!" marveled Mother.

"Yes, and a garden if you want to keep busy outdoors. And a phonograph with nineteen records, musical and comic, by Jiminy!"

To prove which he darted back into the living-room, started "Molly Magee, My Girl," and to its cheerful strains he danced a fantastic jig, while the maid stared from the dining-room, and Mother, at the bedroom door, wept undisguisedly, murmuring, "Oh, my boy, my boy, that planned it all to surprise me!"

SINCLAIR LEWIS

XVIII

Mother had, after an energetic September, succeeded in putting all the furniture to rights and in evoking curtains and linen. Anybody, even the impractical Father, can fill a house with furniture, but it takes two women and at least four weeks to make the furniture look as though it had grown there. She had roamed the fields, and brought home golden-rod and Michaelmas daisies and maple leaves. She no longer panted or felt dizzy when she ran up the stairs. She was a far younger woman than the discreet brown hermit of the dusty New York flat, just as the new Father, who had responsibility and affairs, was younger than the Pilkings clerk of old.

Always she watched for Father's home-coming. He usually came prancing home so happily that, one evening, when Mother saw him slowly plod down the street, his head low, his hands sagging his pockets, she ran out to the porch and greeted him with a despairing, "What is it, Seth?"

"Oh, nothing much." Before he would go on, Father put his arm about her ample waist and led her to the new porch-swing overlooking the raw spaded patch of earth that would be a rose-garden some day— that already, to their imaginations, was brilliant with blossoms and alive with birds.

She observed him mutely, anxiously. He handed a letter to her. It was in their daughter's handwriting:

Dear Papa And Mama

I don't know if this letter will reach you, but have been reading pieces in Saserkopee & N. Y. papers about your goings-on and hear you are at a town called Lipsittsville, oh how could you run away from the beautiful home Harris & I gave you, I am sure if there was anything we didn't do for y'r comfort & happiness you had only to ask & here you go and make us a laughing stock in Saserkopee, we had told everyone you would be at our party & suddenly you up & disappear & it has taken us months to get in touch with you, such a wicked, untruthful lie about friend sick in Boston & all. Harris heard from a traveling salesman, & he agreed with Harris how thoughtless and wilful you are, & he told Harris that you are at this place Lipsittsville, so I will address you there & try & see if letter reaches you & tell you that though you must be ashamed of your conduct by now, we are willing to forgive & forget, I was never one to hold a grudge. I am sure if you had just stopped and thought you would have realized to what worry and inconvenience you have put us, & if this does reach you, by now I guess you will have had enough of being bums or pedestrians or whatever fancy name you call yourself, and be glad to come back to a good home and see if you can't show a little sense as you ought to at your time of life, & just think of what the effect must be on Harry when his very own grand-parents acts this way! If you will telegraph me, or write me if you have not got enough money for telegraphing, Harris will come for you, & we will see what can be done for you. We think and hope that a place can be found for you in the Cyrus K. Ginn Old People's Home, where you can spend your last days, I guess this time you will want to behave yourselves, and Harris & I will be glad to have you at our home from time to time. After all my love & thoughtfulness for you—but I guess I need not say anything more, by this time you will have learned your lesson.

Your loving daughter,
LULU

Father and Mother had sat proudly on their porch the night before, and they had greeted passers-by chattily, like people of substance, people healthy and happy and responsible. Now they shrank on the swing; they saw nothing but Lulu's determined disdain for their youthful naughtiness; heard nothing but her voice, hard, unceasing, commenting, complaining; and the obese and humorless humor of Mr. Harris Hartwig.

"She can't make us go back—confine us in this here home for old folks, can she, legally?" It was Mother who turned to Father for reassurance.

"No, no. Certainly not. . . I don't *think* so." They sat still. They seemed old again.

Just before dinner he started up from the swing, craftily laid his finger beside his nose, and whispered something very exciting and mysterious to Mother, who kept saying: "Yes, yes. Yes, yes. Yes, I'd be willing to. Though it would be hard." Immediately after dinner they walked sedately down the village street, while blackbirds whistled from the pond and children sang ancient chants of play under the arc-lights at corners, and neighbors cried "'Evenin'" to them, from chairs on porches. They called upon the town newspaperman, old Lyman Ford, and there was a conference with much laughter and pounding of knees—also a pitcher of lemonade conjointly prepared by Mrs. S. Appleby and Mrs. L. Ford. Finally the Applebys paraded to the telegraph-office, and to Mr. Harris Hartwig, at Saserkopee, they sent this message:

Come see us when can. Wire at once what day and train. Will meet.

A sodden and pathetic figure, in his notorious blue-flannel shirt, and the suit, or the unsuit, which he had worn into Lipsittsville in the days when he had been a hobo, Father waited for the evening train and for Mr. Harris Hartwig.

Mr. Hartwig descended the car steps like a general entering a conquered province. Father nervously concealed his greasy shirt-front with his left hand, and held out his right hand deprecatingly. Mr. Hartwig took it into his strong, virile, but slightly damp, clasp, and held it (a thing which Father devoutly hated) while he gazed magnanimously into Father's shy eyes and, in a confidential growl which could scarce have been heard farther away than Indianapolis, condescended: "Well, here we are. I'm glad there's an end to all this wickedness and foolishness at last. Where's Mother Appleby?"

"She wasn't feeling jus' like coming," Father mumbled. "I'll take you to her."

"How the devil are you earning a living?"

"Why, the gent that owns the biggest shoe-store here was so kind as to give me sort of work round the store like."

"Yuh, as porter, I'll venture! You might just as well be sensible, for once in your life, Father, and learn that you're past the age where you can insist and demand and get any kind of work, or any kind of a place to live in, that just suits your own sweet-fancy. Business ain't charity, you know, and all these working people that think a business is run just to suit *them*—! And that's why you ought to have been more appreciative of all Lulu did for you—and then running away and bringing her just about to the verge of nervous prostration worrying over you!"

They had left the station, now, and were passing along Maple Avenue, with its glory of trees and shining lawns, the new Presbyterian church and the Carnegie Library. Mr. Hartwig of Saserkopee was getting far too much satisfaction out of his rôle as sage and counselor to notice Maple Avenue. He never had the chance to play that rôle when the wife of his bosom was about.

"Another thing," Mr. Hartwig was booming, as they approached the row of bungalows where the Applebys lived, "you ought to have understood the hardship you were bringing on Mother by taking her away from our care—and you always pretending to be so fond of her and all. I don't want to rub it in or nothing, but I always did say that I was suspicious of these fellows that are always petting and stewing over their wives in public—you can be dead sure that in private they ain't got any more real consideration 'n' thoughtfulness for 'em than—than anything. And you can see for yourself now—Here you are. Why, just one look at you is enough to show you're a failure! Why, my garbage-man wears a better-looking suit than that!"

Though Father felt an acute desire to climb upon a convenient carriage-block and punch the noble Roman head of Mr. Harris Hartwig, he kept silent and looked as meek as he could and encouraged his dear son-in-law to go on.

"We'll try to find some decent, respectable work for you," said Mr. Hartwig. "You'll be at liberty to be away from the Old People's Home for several hours a day, perfect freedom, and perhaps now and then you can help at a sale at a shoe-store. Saserkopee is, as you probably know, the best town of its size in New York, and if you did feel you had to keep in touch with business, I can't for the life of me see why you came clear out here to the West—little dinky town with no prospects or nothing. Why even you, at your age, could turn a few dollars in Saserkopee. 'Course with my influence there I could throw things your way." Then, bitterly, "Though of course I wouldn't expect any thanks!"

They turned a corner, came to a row of new bungalows.

The whole block was filled with motor-cars, small black village ones, but very comfortable and dependable. In a bungalow at the end of the block a phonograph was being loud and cheery.

"Somebody giving a party," Mr. Hartwig oracularly informed Father.

"Why! Sure enough! So somebody is! Yes, yes! It must be my boss. That's where I live. Boss lets us bunk in the dust-bin."

Father's voice was excited, slightly hysterical. Mr. Hartwig looked at him wonderingly. "What do you mean, 'in the dust-bin'?" he asked, in a puzzled way.

"I'll show you," said Father, and in a low, poisonous voice he added certain words which could not be made out, but which sounded curiously like "you great big fat weevily ham!"

"We can't butt into this party," protested Mr. Hartwig, suddenly feeling himself in a strange town, among strangers, as Father took his arm in front of the bungalow where the party was being fearlessly enacted.

"I never knew you to hesitate about butting in before," said Father. "Some day I hope you butt into the Cyrus K. Ginn Home for Old Fossils, but now—"

While Mr. Hartwig followed him in alarm, Father skipped up the steps, jabbed at the push-button. The door opened on the living-room— and on a tableau.

In the center of a group of expensive-looking people stood Mother, gorgeous in a gown like a herald's cloth-of-gold tabard. She was as magnificent as one of the larger chairs in a New York hotel lobby. Her hair was waved. She was coldly staring at Harris through a platinum lorgnon. Round her were the élite of Lipsittsville—the set that wore dinner coats and drove cars. A slim and pretty girl in saffron-colored silk bowed elaborately. A tall man with an imperial chuckled.

"Why, Harris, this is ver', ver' pleasant. I had almost forgotten you were coming," Mother said, languidly. . . Harris could not know that the distinguished pedestrian, actor, impresario, and capitalist, Mr. Seth Appleby, had spent two hours and seventeen minutes in training the unwilling Mother to deliver this speech. If Mother stumbled somewhat as she went on, that merely enhanced her manner of delicate languor: "So pleasant to see you. Just a few of our friends dropped in for a little informal gathering. Would you like to wash up and join us? Seth dear, will you ring for Lena and have her take dear Harris's bag to his room? Did you bring your evening clothes, Harris?"

One time in his life, Harris had rented evening clothes, but otherwise—

They didn't give Harris a chance to ask for explanations. When, still in his dusty bulbous gray sack suit, he hesitated out of his pleasant room, he found that Father had changed to dinner coat and a stock, which he was old enough to wear with distinction. Harris was firmly introduced to Mr. Lyman Ford, sole owner and proprietor of the Lipsittsville *Ozone*. He was backed into a corner, and filled with tidings about the glories of Mr. and Mrs. Seth Appleby, their social position and athletic prowess and financial solidity, and the general surpassing greatness of Lipsittsville. In fact, Mr. Ford overdid it a little, and Mr. Hartwig began to look suspicious—like a man about to sneeze, or one who fears that you are going to try to borrow money from him.

But with an awkward wonder which expressed itself in his growing shyness, his splay-footed awkwardness, his rapidly increasing deference to Father, Mr. Hartwig saw Lena, the maid, spread forth tables for the social and intellectual game of progressive euchre; saw Father combat mightily with that king of euchre-players, Squire Trowbridge; saw the winners presented with expensive-looking prizes. And there were refreshments. The Lipsittsville *Ozone* would, in next Thursday's issue, be able to say, "Dainty refreshments, consisting of angel's-food, ice-cream, coffee, macaroons, and several kinds of pleasing sandwiches, were served."

Miss Mattie Ford, the society editor of the *Ozone*, was at her wittiest during the food-consumption, and a discussion of Roosevelt and the co-operative creamery engaged some of the brightest minds in Lipsittsville. Father, listening entranced, whispered to Mother, as he passed her with his tray of ice-cream, "I guess Harris don't hear any bright talk like this in Saserkopee. Look at him. Goggle-eyed. I always said he looked like a frog. Except that he looks more like a hog."

"I won't have you carrying on and being rude," Mother said, most convincingly.

The party did not end till clear after eleven. When the street was loud with the noise of cars starting, and quantities of ladies in silk wraps laughingly took their departure, Mr. Harris Hartwig stood deserted by the fireplace. When the door had closed on the last of the revelers Father returned, glanced once at him, coldly stopped to pick up a chair which had been upset, then stalked up to Harris and faced him, boring him with an accusing glance.

"Well," said Harris, uneasily, "you sure got—Say, I certainly got to hand it to you, Father Appleby." Like a big, blubbery, smear-faced school-boy he complained, "Gee! I don't think it's fair, making a goat of me this way, when I came to do you a service and take you home and all."

He was so meek that Father took pity on him.

"We'll call it square," he said. "I guess maybe you and Lulu will quit worrying, now, at last."

"Yes, I guess we'll have to. . . Say, Father, this seems to be a fine, live, prosperous town. Say, I wonder what's the chances for opening a drug-store here? Competition is getting pretty severe in Saserkopee."

For the first time since he had married the lovely Lulu Harris Hartwig seemed to care for his father-in-law's opinion.

Father took one horrified glance at Mother. The prospect of the Hartwigs planted here in Eden, like a whole family of the most highly irritating serpents, seemed to have paralyzed her. It was Father who turned Harris's flank. Said he:

"Well, I'm afraid I can't encourage you. There's three good stores here, and the proprietors of all of them are friends of mine, and I'm afraid I couldn't do a thing about introducing you. In fact, I'd feel like a traitor to them if I was responsible for any competition with them. So—But some time, perhaps, we can have Lulu and Harry here for a visit."

"Thank you, Father. Well—"

"Well, I guess we all better be saying good night."

Father ostentatiously wound up the clock and locked the doors. Harris watched him, his Adam's apple prettily rising and falling as he prepared to speak and hesitated, again and again. Finally, as Father yawned and extended his hand, Harris burst out: "Say, how—the—deuce—did you get this house and all? What's the idea, anyway?"

For this Father had been waiting. He had nineteen large batteries concealed in ambush. And he fired them. He fixed Harris with a glance that was the condensed essence of all the fathers-in-law in the world. "Young man," he snorted, "I don't discuss my business affairs. But I don't mind saying that I am partner in one of the most flourishing mercantile concerns in the State. I knew that Lulu and you would never believe that the poor old folks could actually run their own business unless you came and saw for yourself. I stand ready to refund the railroad fare you spent in coming here. Now are you satisfied?"

"Why—why, yes—"

"Well, then, I guess we'll say good night."

"Good night," said Harris, forlornly.

It was a proof of their complete recovery from Harris-Hartwigism that, while they were undressing, the Applebys discussed Mr. Hartwig only for a moment, and that Father volunteered: "I actually do hope that Lulu and Harry will come to pay us a visit now. Maybe we can impress her, too. I hope so. I really would like a chance to love our daughter a little. Don't seem natural we should always have to be scared of her. Well, let's forget the Hartwigs. They'll come around now. Catch them not knowing where their bread is buttered. Why, think, maybe

Lulu will let me kiss her, some day, without criticizing my necktie while I'm doing it!"

The Innocents, the conquering babes in the wood, put out all the lights except the bedside lamp on the table between their twin beds. These aristocratic beds were close enough together so that they could lie with their out-stretched hands clasped. They had left the door into the living-room open, and the low lights from the coals in the fireplace made a path across the polished floor and the new rugs—a vista of spaciousness and content.

"It's our first real home," murmured Father. "My old honey, we've come home! We'll have the Tubbses here from the Cape, come Christmas-time. Yes, and Crook McKusick, if we ever hear from him! And we'll play cribbage. I bet I can beat Joe Tubbs four games out of five. Say, look here, young woman, don't you go to sleep yet. I'm a hard-working man, and it's Doc Schergan's orders that I got to be played with and hold your hand like this for fourteen minutes every night, before I go to sleep. . . My old honey!"

"How you do run on!" said Mother, drowsily.

THE END

A Note About the Author

Sinclair Lewis (1885–1951) was an American author and playwright. As a child, Lewis struggled to fit in with both his peers and family. He was much more sensitive and introspective than his brothers, so he had a difficult time connecting to his father. Lewis' troubling childhood was one of the reasons he was drawn to religion, though he would struggle with it throughout most of his young adult life, until he became an atheist. Known for his critical views of American capitalism and materialism, Lewis was often praised for his authenticity as a writer. With over twenty novels, four plays, and around seventy short stories, Lewis was a very prolific author. In 1930, Sinclair Lewis became the first American to receive the Nobel Prize for literature, setting an inspiring precedent for future American writers.

A Note from the Publisher

Spanning many genres, from non-fiction essays to literature classics to children's books and lyric poetry, Mint Edition books showcase the master works of our time in a modern new package. The text is freshly typeset, is clean and easy to read, and features a new note about the author in each volume. Many books also include exclusive new introductory material. Every book boasts a striking new cover, which makes it as appropriate for collecting as it is for gift giving. Mint Edition books are only printed when a reader orders them, so natural resources are not wasted. We're proud that our books are never manufactured in excess and exist only in the exact quantity they need to be read and enjoyed.

Discover more of your favorite classics with Bookfinity™.

- Track your reading with custom book lists.
- Get great book recommendations for your personalized Reader Type.
- Add reviews for your favorite books.
- AND MUCH MORE!

Visit **bookfinity.com** and take the fun Reader Type quiz to get started.

Enjoy our classic and modern companion pairings!